And to Mom and Dad for believing *in me.*

THIS GIRL CLIMBS TREES

by Ellen Plotkin Mulholland

LOGOS PUBLISHING HOUSE
BERKELEY

This Girl Climbs Trees
A Logos Publishing House book

Createspace edition published December 2012
Logos Publishing House edition published October 2013

Library of Congress Control Number: 2013913292
Mulholland, Ellen Plotkin
ISBN-13: 978-0989745512
ISBN-10: 0989745511
Fiction
Printed in the United States of America

This is a work of fiction. Names, characters, places and incidents are either products of the author's imagination or are used fictitiously. Any resemblance to actual events or locales or persons, living or dead, is entirely coincidental.

After all, life is simply a series of possibilities yet unseen. Life is a story to be written.

LOGOS
PUBLISHING
HOUSE

WWW.LOGOSPUBLISHINGHOUSE.COM

www.logospublishinghouse.com

What follows...

You are about to step inside my head. These are my thoughts, my worries, my fears, my excitements. I don't just invite anyone inside my head. Yes, you should feel privileged.

Maybe you keep a journal, a diary, or something. It's a great way to get out all that stuff that just jumbles inside us. I think so, anyway. Being a teenager isn't easy, but talking to someone about all those crazy thoughts sure does help.

So I'm gonna talk to you.

Thanks for listening.

I'll see you inside...

0

NOT YOUR EVERYDAY TREE-CLIMBER

January 1979, age 13 and two months(ish)

I'm not afraid of climbing trees. I once cherished a majestic maple that stood solidly on our front lawn, guarding the house like some armored knight. That maple was the first tree I ever climbed but not the last. Still, it will forever be my favorite. My first best friend.

No other tree on the block stood taller, leafier, or greener in spring, nor turned as many beautiful shades of orange and brown in fall. If there were an award for the most beautiful climbing tree in Santa Nina, California, the Mills' maple would surely have won, hands down.

Its bumpy brown trunk provided nature's best stepladder up to my favorite branch. This gentle long arm extended lovingly toward my bedroom window inviting me to climb up the tree onto its sturdy branch any given sunny day, just to lie on my stomach, arms dangling, denim-covered legs bent at the knees, crossed at the ankles, and feet clothed only by dirt and sap.

Somehow, my pixie-cut brown hair seemed always to invite a few stray leaves. Never in all my years have I experienced more bliss than on the motherly limb of that maple tree.

Tree-lying started when I was eight and ended three

years later when it became tree-sitting because the hard branch hurt my new, my changing, my (you know, b-o-o-you know). Dad had the tree uprooted two weeks before I turned 13, said it had some sort of terminal disease.

Such are the problems of the female tree-lyer.

The name on my birth certificate reads Maclyn Elizabeth Mills, but ever since I can remember, people have called me Mac. Then last year I started signing homework Eliza Mills, Esq. I decided I deserved a bit of moving up in this world. (Didn't matter to me that esquire is meant for boys.) And if the only way I could do it was by changing my name, so be it. I don't think my family thinks much of it. In fact, Eric's the only one who calls me Eliza.

Here's the silly naming story. Everyone has one. This is mine.

Dad: Let's name our only little girl after a beautiful woman, Jacqueline Bouvier Kennedy Onassis.
Mom: How about after my best friend from high school; you know, the one who killed herself when she didn't make the cheer squad. Madeline.
Me (had I a voice): This is kinda morbid people. Sure, I get the intent and all, but come on, a little compassion.
Parents: Why don't we combine the two names? Yeah. Maclyn. Sounds kinda like a fish, but it's the sentiment behind it all.

See why I prefer my second name, Elizabeth? Eliza. I think it sounds so much more grown up. Because as hard as I try to convince myself that a name is a name is a name, I just can't fall in love with MACLYN. Doesn't Eliza sound better? Maybe you have a name that doesn't please you. I say, change it. Remember, you are the one (not your sappy parents) who has to go through life with it. I think that by age 13, I ought to be able to call myself whatever I want.

This is my life so far. And because of some recently developing events, I felt an urge, maybe a calling, to share my world with, well, with the world. It's funny that what is helping me understand life right now is death. That's just wrong.

What's it all about, anyway? Life. Deep thought like this calls for an elevated view of the world. That's why I'm a tree-climber.

Now I'm not your everyday tree-climber. It's a whole kind of out-of-this-world experience for me. Foot to bark, hand to twig, and body to branch sends me into some other place. It's like the tree and me are one. I trust the tree to hold me; the tree trusts me not to chop it down.

Surely, it won't hold my dad's insanity and one sharp axe of Tim's Lumber against me. Will it?

As far as I can tell at this point, there're just a few things you need for this twisted journey of life. Start with a belief in yourself, a trust of your own instincts and a dash of honesty - no, not a dash, a heaping tablespoon - because if you're not honest with you, your instincts will lie, and then you've had it.

Trusting your instincts and climbing trees share a common truth – you don't know anything until you try. You won't know if your instincts lie or if you can't climb a tree unless you take that first step. And always remember tree-climbing rule number one:

No Tree's Too Tall

Those aren't the words of some ancient mystic. They're my words. The words of a sometimes confused 13-year-old girl, daughter of a behind-the-times dad and one lipstick-wearing mom, sister of four very protective brothers, and best friend to the smartest girl on the West Coast.

I take what life hands me and move forward. So what that the cutest guy on the block might not like girls. So what that

Joe Basketball still thinks playing sports is the ultimate way to spend his time. So what if I take the world seriously. So what.

It's the world that better watch out. Not me.

1

THE IMPORTANCE OF TREES

There must be more to this world than simply growing, more to life than just living. What's the importance of me, the importance of a friendship formed then torn apart?

My first friendship crossed species, as do many important childhood relationships. My first true friend never yelled at me, took my toys, or excluded me from fun and games. My first friend waited for me everyday outside my window.

A tree sprouts from the ground into a mighty figure. A girl toddles barefoot across the cool summer grass, sporting a bright yellow-polka-dot sundress, and heads straight toward this sentinel. A first attraction for figures tall and strong.

My mighty maple began its life long before I arrived. Dad said they bought our house mostly because of the tree's chosen position on the front lawn. The top branches already tickled the roof's edges, and my mom immediately took to the shade its leaves would provide the baby's room in summer.

That baby was me.

I arrived in the fall of 1965. My mom remembers rocking me by the window as the mighty maple shed its leaves like snowfall. My brothers might not have shared her poetic sigh, though, as they were the ones to rake and pack the fallen crispy soldiers for three weeks straight. By the time I entered kindergarten, I was part of the leaf-packing team. One giggling girl and her four big brothers, raking, packing, and some major leaf diving.

There's definitely an importance to trees, in climbing them. Something is learned in this feat that can't be taught in classrooms, can't be passed on by parents, can't be written about in books.

Kenny, my oldest brother by eight years, taught me how to climb. Although he preferred tackling the trunk in sneakers, I instinctively threw off my shoes and began my first ascent barefoot. He had marked out a path for me – literally. With a black crayon, he circled the bumpy points where I could lodge a foot or grab on with my hands.

The first time Kenny stood behind me and pushed my bottom up as I strained with all my determined 8-year-old power. After about four feet, I reached the first limb and pulled myself up. Seemed more like a hugging than a climbing. I wrapped my arms around the trunk and shimmied, scooted, pushed and gripped until I reached a nook – that elbow where limb meets trunk.

What a memorable and glorious moment. Hugging the thick extended branch like a pillow, rubbing my hands along its smooth bark and over small bumps, memorizing her form, her imperfections that so perfectly graced her. She wore notches and scars like jewels to a party.

Once I achieved the climb without Kenny's behind support, it became something of an obsession. Home from school and straight up that tree. Saturday morning after a bowl of Froot Loops, straight up my tree. Summer-free livin' and, well, you get the picture.

Nothing beat it. Especially in the summertime when its cool bark soothed my sun-toasted skin. By age ten, I managed to climb to the next limb – the one that reached straight toward my bedroom window.

Such a true sense of accomplishment and magic cannot be fully described - the emotional uplift I felt in that shining moment. Its fleeting memory lives deep inside me, inside a place indescribable and beautiful. I close my eyes, and I am there, in that nook, bottom propped back against the trunk, legs straddling her limb and wrapped tight at the ankles, arms hugging her and not letting go. Sitting up I could almost reach my window just a feet away. Turning my head I stared straight at my neighbors' rooftops. I spied a red rubber ball on the Gold's and faded green Frisbee on the Park's.

I open my eyes, and find myself smiling at memories that remain now just that: memories inside one teenage girl's mind.

Just three short years after I'd made it to that second limb, my dad let me know that my maple had a disease.

October 1978, age 12, 11 months, two weeks, home

"There's some infestation, Mac, it's going around. See the white streaks?" he pointed at her trunk, just above the base.

I stared at nothing. "Where? I don't see anything but bark."

"It's there," he assured me. "Trust me, Mac, we've got to chop her down. Tim's Lumber said they could still salvage her timber. He'll pay for the clean-up if we donate her."

Two weeks to my 13th birthday and this was my present into teendom – losing my tree. I stroked her firm, loving trunk. I swallowed, cleared my throat. "Can't we get medicine? Isn't there some kind of tree vitamin or something?"

"No, Honey, it's too late for that." My towering dad dwarfed under my mighty maple. His fireman's shoulders sagged, revealing his misgivings at sharing this news. "Come on, Mac, you're about to turn 13. It's time to stop climbing trees anyway. You should be focusing on girl stuff."

I believe I actually stopped breathing at his words. "Girl stuff? What's that supposed to mean?" *Girl stuff.* "Dad, I've been climbing this tree for almost five years. She's part of my childhood, part of me, Dad. You can't just chop her down and expect me to just say OKAY, time to grow up and be a girl!" Unaware of the tears streaming down my face or the fists gripping at the ends of my arms, I shouted, "I hate you, you can't do this!"

I ran and ran, not inside to my mother, not to my best friend's, I just ran. Time stopped. I leaped over hoses, crossed streets without looking, darted through parked cars in driveways, and finally threw myself down on some unknown around-the-corner neighbor's lawn.

Lying face down with my hands wiping tears, I bawled like a baby. Then just as suddenly, I gasped and gasped and stopped. I sat up. Expecting to see my dad, I saw no one.

I breathed in and out, calming myself. Reality hit. I couldn't save my maple. Looking up toward the October sky, I observed wispy clouds stretched across its blueness. I breathed again, pulled my knees into my chest and wrapped my arms around myself. Two weeks to teenage life and I was losing my first best friend.

I stood and marched in a solitary funeral procession back home where I could sit with my tree one last time.

Eric, the smartest of my four older brothers, has always told me that every part of life has its own special meaning and purpose. If you just sit and listen, answers come to you. You don't have to go looking for them. So, I'm waiting ... and ... nothing.

If the answer to what life's all about is death, loss, tragedy, you can keep that. Losing my beagle Snoopy to a racing car, my neighbor Benjie to more insanity, and now my maple – each sits inside me like an undigested seed at the pit of my stomach. Dormant seeds not wanting, not able, to grow or sprout into anything but sorrow.

Eric says I'm not seeing the BIGGER picture. So, I'm

looking, putting on my magic glasses and peering into life's microscope. (Actually, maybe I should be looking through binoculars – see close up what's so far away.) It's not merely my tree that I mourn, there's more.

Snap out of it, you say? I'm trying, believe me.

Fortunately, I have another best friend. Paisley Park. She helps me sort out confusions. She moved in next door the day after my neighbor Benjie's accident.

I wish I could say it was the day that changed my life. Maybe it was, but that's not how you see things when you're four years old. Still, Pais has had a big effect on me.

Besides sharing the same Zodiac, all we really have in common is our desire to grow up as soon as possible.

Growing up – *God's little joke?* I mean, adults always say that they'd never want to go through their teen years again. (That's encouraging.)

"They just didn't know what they were doing," says Paisley. "You've got to trust your instincts." Pais believes that our instincts are All That Is (God/Goddess) talking. Actually, what she says is: "She speaks to us, through us, just listen, the voices you hear, the loving ones, the ones giving you the right advice – that's the Goddess, All That Is."

Listen to your intuition, your instincts. Makes sense. Someone must know the plan. Why not an invisible force that whispers in your ear?

*   *   *

Invisible whispers, sudden ideas out of the blue, helpful strangers – I will take them all, because right now I'm in the middle of a crisis.

Just weeks after losing my maple, I lost my Grandpa. It's been more than a month, but it still feels like it happened yesterday. I wanted to stop writing. Stop thinking. Just stop. Completely.

No one prepared me for this. No one told me that death

could be so wicked, so thoughtless. That when someone you love dies, it's absolutely rotten.

I thought no pain could hurt more than the gooey glob that filled my heart the day Tim's Lumber carted away my maple on the back of that rusty green flatbed, her trunk chopped into 11 pieces, her lovely limbs tossed carelessly over her dismembered body. Leafless twigs and skinny branches scattered our lawn.

I was wrong. Losing your grandpa is different.

Uncle Bert flew in, and he and Mom drove down to Las Palimas to help Grandma. We drove down a few days later for a small funeral, just family. Grandpa wanted to be cremated and have his ashes spread across the desert. So we did that.

Now Mom's out in New York helping Grandma settle in with Uncle Bert. I like that she's back with her son. I just don't want Grandma to be lonely.

I wonder if there are a lot of trees in New York City. I mean, sure, in Central Park, but what about away from there? Does Uncle Bert have a sturdy maple growing outside his apartment? Do they even have maple trees in New York City? And if they do, who climbs them?

How's a girl like me to grow roots when the soil of life is so crumbly?

Perhaps growing up isn't something to learn but something to do. So on I go, growing up now without my maple, my grandpa or any idea of what I'm doing.

2

SEASON OF CHANGE

Mom's been in New York for three days now. She didn't call last night, so I'll just have to assume everything's OKAY. The first night she arrived, she told me that Grandma wanted to send back some important things to us. Mom didn't know what, but she said I shouldn't expect it to be anything more than trinkets.

Trinkets to Mom, maybe. To me, they might be treasures. For sure they will be memories. There are so many possibilities of what a grandmother might want to send home to her grandchildren. All I know is that whatever they are, I will cherish them.

I feel that sense of cherishing things more often lately. After all, it's the New Year, I'm 13, and everyone's talking about resolutions and changing how they do things.

Why change what you love?

Anyway, this is not the time of year that's best for making resolutions.

Fall's the time. Definitely fall.

Fall, so beautiful. Staring out my bedroom window and following the floating path of each falling leaf from my maple. That's a memory. A memory to cherish.

Fall is the *Change Season*. Not just of leaves but of everything. We always think January First calls for the beginning of something new, but it comes in the middle of winter. How can one begin something new with cloudy skies and a nose running faster than Carl Lewis? It's difficult enough trying to make it to school when it's pouring rain outside and you'd rather stay snuggled up in your nice warm bed, let alone having to think up five New Year's resolutions.

Santa Nina, California, isn't exactly the best – definitely not the most cheerful – place to be in the winter.

Mom never lets me stay home on those soggy days. Maybe if she did, I would be able to think up some clever resolutions. Fall inspires so much more change. When everything outside you is changing, you want to change. Fall inspires *me*.

Leaves gradually turn from green to brown. The glowing sun dims its brilliant shine. Summer vacation ends, a new school year begins. Sunny days grow shorter, darker, making way for quiet amber days. See you later playful summer sounds.

Not that poetic, you say? At the next change of season, observe the trees, the landscapes of your city, a park - listen, look, feel. Perhaps then you'll agree. Fall is inspirational.

Of course, my brothers don't see it this way. (Except maybe Eric. "Just breathe it in, Eliza, inhale the change, the leaves, the crisp air. Ahhh. I love that coldness that fills my chest. Do you feel that, Sis?") The rest of my brothers don't just dislike fall because they have to return to school, but because the girls stop wearing shorts and sleeveless dresses.

"Why cover up a beautiful girl in layers of wool?" Marc will say.

"Yeah, what's up with layers, Man?" might return any one of his shallow friends. Bulky sweaters, jeans and galoshes are another reason I prefer fall. No more skimpy revealing clothing.

Summer then remains the most sexist season: bikinis,

mini-skirts, halter-tops, and shorts.

Fall, however, enters and one's whole environment begins to change, so you have this unique opportunity to shift, if not simply turn on an inside view of your inner world. You see, the other seasons remain the same throughout their months.

Summer stays hot and dry, winter just the opposite, and spring flaunts its flower-inducing sneezing attacks. Fall's picture constantly moves as the leaves begin their descent in hue, as well as height, the grass loses its bright green coat, and flowers in bloom begin to die. The air gradually cools, the winds grow fiercer and chillier, and the skies cloudier.

Fall is the perfect moment in time for change.

The only real thing that interrupts such serious thoughts during fall is school. You can't quite take time out to "put your life in perspective" when you have a geography exam in the morning or a pig to dissect in fourth period.

In fact, it's hard to keep my mind on school right now when I miss my grandpa and my maple. I feel empty inside like the branch of a tree. I wrap myself in soft sweaters and spray myself with Baby Soft just to keep my senses alive.

Here I am at 13, the world before me, and I'm feeling down. This just won't do. Time to shift my thoughts to something more constructive. I need to lift myself out of this mud and expand my world.

What I need is a distraction.

3

MY BEST FRIEND (AND HER CUTE BROTHER)

OKAY, Mom just called. Sounds like things are settling. She'll be home in a few days. Grandma still talks as if Grandpa is alive. I guess that's normal. I wonder if she talks to his ashes? (She kept some, you know.)

When I heard that Grandpa wanted to be cremated, I was kind of creeped out.

He assured me, "It's the best way to do it. God only wants the soul, Maclyn. He's no use for this worn down old body."

Still, I can't help but think it hurts to be burned. Eric says I think that because I "identify too much" with my body. Well, yeah, I kind of like having one.

I wonder if they took out his false teeth. Or if they placed his cane with him. Or his bifocals. I wonder if they took the tubes out in the hospital. Or if they burned him in that ghostly white hospital gown, or in his favorite brown cardigan, the one with the mustard stains.

I wonder what Grandpa's last thoughts were. His last feelings? Was he afraid? At the very end. Did he even know what was happening? At the very end.

I wonder if, if Grandpa was happy. If he had had any

regrets. Anything he wished he'd done. Wished he hadn't.

Can he hear me right now? *Hey, Grandpa, do you know that I really loved you, really? I love you still, right now. Are you happy up there, Grandpa? Can you see me?*

Hey, Grandpa, have you met God? Do they have maple trees in Heaven?

I wonder if Grandpa ever knew anything about it coming. At the very end. Felt anything. Sensed anything. If he's just plain dead right now. Without wings. Just dead.

Why do people we love the most die before we've really told them about all the love we have for them?

Writing all of this keeps my mind occupied. My thoughts fill my head, while my feelings stand aside. It's not how Paisley would handle death. But I'm not Paisley.

Okay, maybe I should try to take my mind off Grandpa. I guess this as good a time as any to give the real scoop on my second best friend in the whole world - Paisley Emma Park. Sometimes, I think that when God/Goddess thought up Pais, She designed her just for me.

Paisley came into my life just as my little neighbor Benjie left it.

Four-year-olds probably bounce when they walk. However, I just can't imagine Paisley Park bouncing. No pigtails adorned that tot's head. Free as a day, hair flyin', knees dirty, and most likely carrying something of purpose. A crayon. A pot. A coloring book. Maybe some play keys. There is no way the girl I know today ever carried a doll.

But memories are funny things, and mine tells me that my best friend did step out of that wood-paneled station wagon with a tiny red-headed rag doll in her arms that sunny June day. Even though it all makes sense to me that way, Paisley denies it.

"A doll? Really. I've never owned a doll. Those are for

girls. I mean, for, you know, girls who want to be mommies." Can you hear her upturned nose?

The summer of 1970, just four going on five, our neighbors, the Kellys, had sold their house and moved to Texas. The Parks seemed to arrive literally hours after the house was cleared out. (At least that's how my mom tells it.)

"They looked so sure of themselves," my mom once recalled. "And such free birds. Bob and Linda practically wore those denim overalls for two weeks straight, unloading boxes, painting the eaves on the side of the house, and you and Paisley, instant friends. Instant. I brought over a lime Jello mold to welcome them the day after the moving van arrived, and you handed Paisley one of your Kiddles. I couldn't believe it. One of your more intact dolls with the cutest little outfit. And you know what that little four-year-old did?" This part drove my mom nuts. "She looked at it and said, 'Dolls are for girls. I'm gonna be a boss. You keep it. You don't look like a boss.'"

I've reminded Paisley of this story several times. She thinks my mom misheard her. Yeah, so what did she say then?

"How should I know," Paisley always says. "I was four. Anyway, maybe I did say something like that. You *don't* look like a boss."

Then we'd laugh, because there is no way Paisley's parents, Bob and Linda, would ever intentionally raise their child to be a boss.

Last of the fanatical Sixties hippie wannabes; you see, Paisley's grandparents grew up in California and raised Linda in a kind of community home where everyone shared a backyard and families traded off cooking and stuff. So she kind of has this attitude that every child is part hers. To Paisley's mom, I'm her "other daughter".

When you walk through the Park's front door, it's like

going through a time machine. Nothing but the voices of John Lennon, Bob Dylan and Joni Mitchell escape their stereo. There's always some sweet incense burning, candles glowing. This den of peace doesn't compare to my house where you trip over some kind of ball or bat or hat everywhere you turn.

Pais tolerates her home, for the most part - even the multi-colored love beads hanging from every doorway. At first, she protested the dangling plastic balls, saying they deprived her of a girl's privacy. So Bob and Linda (who believe everyone deserves a say in everything) didn't argue. Paisley's doorway now remains dangle-free. Still, I don't think they're as cool as they'd like people to believe.

"Everyone has the right to happiness," spouts Bob. "No one should have a life of pure luxury while others sleep in the streets. No one has the right to trample on the underprivileged."

The next thing you know, Bob motors up their driveway in his pristine midnight blue BMW convertible, returning from a day at his soda company public relations job. Linda spends most afternoons with society ladies and charity work.

It's like they live one life in the house and another on the street. Who are the real Bob and Linda?

I suppose I should relax and just allow life's contradictions to rest undisturbed. Paisley always tells me to stop trying to make the world perfect because, in a way, the world is perfect; but in another way, it never can be the perfect we want it to be.

What Paisley's parents don't realize is that all of their free-will talk has rubbed off quite a bit on their only daughter. She has taken to heart every word. Really, though, I think she's a bit confused: should she follow their wise words or copy their practical actions?

Actually, unlike me, Pais doesn't get as frustrated with these choices. She listens to her inner voice.

"God/Goddess will lead me in the right direction. I just need to listen."

I'd rather listen to her cute brother John F. Yeah, you guessed it, named for one and the same. No not named actually, it's just another one of those coincidences.

He was born before Kennedy ran for the White House. John F used to go by Johnny. But after 1961, when he turned four, his parents started calling him John F because they said they sensed a great calm in him as in their beloved president. The F here stands for Franklin – Johnathan Franklin Parks. Even his name is dreamy!

Pais doesn't have any sisters – just like me. John F is her only sibling. How lucky am I to witness his incredible smile everyday? I watch dreamily as he enters the kitchen, muddied jeans, torn in just the right spot at his knee, revealing enough skin to hint at his softness.

Lost in a daydream, I rarely hear his "Hey, Mac,"when he passes me. I'm too busy smelling the sweet grass stains and boy sweat. I catch his flashy grin as he turns his head, perspiration-dripping strands of hair flying across his forehead. He grabs a box of Frosted Flakes from the cupboard, and he's gone.

"Eliza, hey, are you listening? Hello, earth to Eliza..."

"Ow! Hey, why'd you pinch me?" I snap at Paisley, unaware of the last three minutes of conversation she had tried to engage me in.

Like most sisters, Paisley pays little attention to her all-star good-looking brother. In fact, I don't know why I even bother. John F would never find me – nor any other girl – interesting, in that way. He's the same age as my brother Kenny, but they aren't good friends like Pais and me.

I think John F wanted to be friends with Kenny, but

Kenny wasn't into that, you know. God, JF is such a fox! Maybe, when he sees me all grown up, in three or four years, he'll change his mind back to girls.

One can dream.

Pais knows nothing of my secret crush on her only brother. We don't usually keep secrets from each other; I just haven't told her. (To be honest, boys have never been a primary topic of conversation between the two of us.) Sometimes, she makes fun of my ideas, or things I do.

Paisley Park is never short on opinions. I bet she had ideas about her future from the moment she was born. When she and I first started talking about what we wanted to be when we grew up, she wanted to be a child psychiatrist. She was nine.

Now, a much-matured 13, she wants to lead a social revolution against the American government. That little seed probably began sprouting out of some past birthday gifts from her folks.

For her twelfth birthday, October 27, 1977, Pais got two history books on Vietnam. The year before, it was a two-year subscription to *Newsweek* magazine. I tried to read one issue and couldn't follow a thing. I'm not even going to open those Vietnam books.

This idea of a revolution invades Paisley's every thought. We organized the secret society in charge of the reform the summer before we turned 11. By default, I'd be what you'd call a founding member.

Now, don't start calling Washington. This is no big movement. In a way, I believe this is Paisley's process of sorting through those contradictions. She wants to be part of change in this country, just like her parents, but she also wants to lead people to happiness.

I think for you to best understand the child-like innocence of this "club" and of Paisley, we need to return to the summer of 1976, six years of a developing lifelong friendship later.

Not quite 11 - still considered kids - Pais and I suddenly awoke to a post-Vietnam world where not every neighbor flew his flag on July 4th.

Our purpose in life knocked loudly on the door. So with utter naivety, we opened it.

4

HEADQUARTERS, SHAG CARPETS, AND CHOCOLATE CHIP COOKIES

Our headquarters leave little to brag about. I would love to describe in detail the damp wooden tree house we hide in to conduct our secret meetings, how the roof leaks in winter and ants collect on the floor in summer. How we spend cold nights arranging devilish plans, or how people try to peak in, curiously wondering what's going on inside.

But that tree house doesn't exist.

Our hideout (if one can even call it that) remains quite unglamorous, plain, and boring. In the winter, central heating warms our toes; in the summer, air conditioning cools our foreheads; year-round, wall-to-wall graduating blue tones of shag carpet brush past our hands, and plates of home-baked chocolate chip cookies flow freely from the Park's electric oven.

Paisley's blue and white bedroom serves as our secret clubhouse. We discuss all-important matters there. Any confidential notes exchanged between us and all minutes from the meetings quietly hide in a shoebox inside my bedroom one house over.

It may not impress James Bond, but it serves our purpose well.

1976, age 10 and a half, the Park's home

Apparently, Pais had been planning the organization in her head for a year. Then finally, one sticky Santa Nina night after a hot summer's rain, July 1976, Pais called me on the phone and beckoned me over. That evening we conducted the organization's first meeting. (That same July evening when her parents discussed the possibility of our former California governor making a run for President of the United States.) An actor in the white house ruffled Paisley's nearly 11-year-old feathers.

After Linda let me in and proceeded through all the "how're your folks" and "you're getting taller every day, Maclyn" mumbo jumbo, I hurried upstairs to Paisley's room. The door shut, I knocked lightly.

"Who's there?" shouted an accusatory - and might I add, paranoid - Paisley, like something out of MacBeth.

"It's me, Pais, Eliza." I tried turning the knob. Locked? "Let me in, will ya?"

Paisley opened her door, pulled me in then peered out into the empty hall before shutting and re-locking the *fort*. I glanced at a pamphlet on her bed, *Animal Liberation*. A blank writing pad and black Bic pen lay beside it.

"What's going on, Pais? What's the emergency?"

"Shh." She picked up the pad and pen, gave me a blue pen, and motioned me to join her on the floor. It was after nine, and as far as my parents knew, I was in bed asleep. I had snuck out my window and climbed down my maple. Pais knew I had to get back quickly, so she wasted no time getting to the point.

We are about to organize a revolution, she wrote in her straight-up-and-down printing. And, as became customary in our meetings for the first year, every word exchanged was written on the pad. I've been thinking about this for a year and have decided tonight's the night we begin.

She handed me the pad. I read it then looked up at her quizzically, smiled, and, not quite knowing what to say, watched Paisley snatch the pad back.

WHAT DO YOU THINK, ELIZA? she wrote boldly. She lifted the pen slightly, peered up at me. I had been reading her words upside down and could make out everything she had written. My stomach gurgled – perhaps in protest – still digesting Mom's London Broil.

I took the pad. *It's a good idea. I guess.*

Pais stared at me, tapping the pen against her mouth and biting her lower lip. We've talked about how bad it feels to eat animals. Remember the TV show about the farmers? How those chickens lived in tiny cages and just laid eggs all day? And how sad those cows looked all crammed together in that truck ready to be killed?

It's time to stop eating meat. Starting tonight. I read an article at the doctor's yesterday about not eating meat. It's called vegetarianism. Lots of people do it. It's safe and healthy. This will be our cause. We will get people to stop killing animals for food and clothing. You know, we don't need to. The Indians did it because they had to survive. Now, we can make clothes from plants, cotton and stuff. What do you say? Are you with me?

I read this carefully then wrote, *Yes*. Paisley looked up and smiled. I added: *I'll stop eating hamburgers and fish and everything. I don't like seeing animals like that either. What do I tell my mom? She says I have to eat meat.*

Your mom doesn't know what she's talking about, wrote my ten-and-a-half year-old friend. I'll get us some pamphlets from the library. You know, we never eat steak, and the doctor says I am in 'tip-top shape'. Just don't tell your folks for a while. When your mom is making the grocery list, tell her you want to try spinach lasagna or something. Tell her you're bored of beef all the time. Make up something. But whatever you do, don't tell your parents about our organization. When school starts up, tell them you've decided to be a vegetarian. Then do really well in school, which you always do anyway, and they won't worry.

Paisley's cleverness amazed me. She had it all worked out. I'm too lazy to devise such creative plans. I'd still be feeling sorry for animals and eating them at the same time. Her plan made perfect sense.

As I was about to write Pais a compliment, she grabbed the pad.

Now, we need to recruit some more girls, trustworthy ones. Here's how it will go - they must be girls, born the same year as us, and definitely vegetarians.

She set down her pen, handed me the pad to read, left the room, and returned moments later with two glasses of milk and a plate of warm freshly baked chocolate chip cookies. We toasted glasses, drank the milk, and ate all 12 cookies.

And so that night began our secret organization.

We've never had more than the six of us. Honestly, the organization is starting to fizzle as everyone's thinking more about high school. No worries. I'm sure Paisley will devise a new club on campus. Isn't that what high school's all about anyway - sharing your views and getting as many people as possible to join you?

You see, my friendship with Paisley rests on more than your typical girl talk. She's been a big influence on me. I know that. Grandpa thinks she's been *too much* of an influence.

I miss Grandpa. It's been more than a month now. It's not like you can buy a new Grandpa in the store, or plant a seed. He's gone for good.

And the memories? It seems that just as I was about to get to know him, it'd be time to go home or to bed or something. Always something.

He and Grandma spent lots of time with the boys. Grandpa did especially. Taking them to ball games, the park, bowling. When I came along all pink and fragile, he didn't know what to do with me.

He loved going to my baseball games and giving me tips. He and Dad would argue over how a "girl should hold a bat". (Why would it be any different from a boy?) I think they just argued to argue.

When I stopped playing, Grandpa didn't have anything much else to say to me. By the time I turned 11, Grandpa had begun his in and out of the hospital visits. By last September, the doctors said he had to stay for good. Grandpa never really got to learn about our organization. Something tells me he would have liked it.

It's just not fair that for the last year or so of his life, Grandpa lay in a hospital bed, tubes sticking out of him, and his only companion a square white machine that looked like a TV sitting at his bedside bleeping reliably on the minute. Maybe he'd gotten used to the whole set-up after awhile.

I suppose anyone might. But life is for living, not getting used to. I don't think I can ever get used to not having my tree or not having my grandpa.

5

TO EVERYTHING, TURN, TURN

The last time I saw Grandpa was just after Thanksgiving, three days before he would die. We had a very long, private conversation, unlike all the times before. For several months, Mom and I had been visiting him every other week.

Sometimes, he'd be too tired or in too much pain to even speak to us. Sometimes, he'd just sleep while Mom sat quietly at his side not saying a word the whole visit. Sometimes, when he was awake, she'd read little items from the newspaper, or a letter from Bert. Or she would just tell him a story. Dad would only visit once a month. Kenny would go on his own about the same, sometimes with Kevin. Eric hardly visited at all. He and Grandpa hadn't gotten along ever since Eric ran away with that religious group. Dad and Grandpa had never gotten on that well, either.

See, Grandpa and Grandma were big church people. They'd go every Sunday and most holidays. That's how Mom grew up. When she and Dad married, she stopped going. I guess being out of Grandpa's home meant to her she could do what she wanted.

I guess Mom didn't like church. Dad never went anyway. Grandpa resented Dad for this. He'd tell Mom she was just doing what her husband did and was still not thinking for herself. That might be true, but looking at Mom, she just doesn't come off as real religious.

Dad tried to explain things to Grandpa, telling him Mom made her own choices, that he wasn't stopping her from anything, she could go to church, a synogogue, whatever. This past year, Dad even tried to be friends with Grandpa, visiting him in the hospital, but Grandpa was too stubborn. Right up to the end.

Ever since Dad's parents died when he was 20, I think he looked forward to getting a "new" dad in Grandpa. But Grandpa wouldn't play that.

I bet that if Dad had got Mom to go to church, it'd be a different story. But that just wouldn't have sat right with Mom or Dad.

So most visits consisted of Mom and me, sometimes Marc. Grandpa liked Marc, but I think he liked Kenny the best, being first-born son and all. Grandpa liked Marc, because he made him laugh.

Towards the end, though, even getting Grandpa to laugh got harder. Towards the end, I'm afraid Grandpa was in a lot of pain. I could see it on his face and Mom's.

Besides our love for Grandpa, I don't think Mom and I have much in common. We rarely speak to each other about anything other than what clothes I need or the trouble of little girls. You'd think in an all-male family such as mine I'd cling to my mom.

Back to that fatal night of October 1978, age 12, home

When I think about it, I feel more connection to my maple than to my mom. She never approved much of my tree climbing. I think she even took a little relief in that invisible disease traveling up my protector's trunk.

"It's a majestic maple and belongs right there on our front lawn," I had cried to her that October night. "Dad can't have it cut down. It's a member of the family."

"Eliza, it's a tree. It's sick. We need to get rid of it before it falls down on the house. What would you think of that, a *murdering maple*?" A morbid attempt at humor.

"Mom, that's not even funny." No one was going to deprive me of my tantrum.

"Okay, you're right. But remember how you used to love to string words together like that? Magic maple. Monkeyboy Marc. Particular Paisley."

"Yeah," I sniffed. Then I remembered one she never liked. "Elegant Eliza."

"Why not Miraculous Maclyn?"

She knew it would never work. I was on my path to a life of Eliza not Maclyn. She ran her cool fingers across my tormented forehead. "You have to let go, Honey. Nothing lasts forever. Your tree is sick and we need to chop it down."

I sighed, readjusted my bangs, and stuffed my hands into my jean pockets. "I just hate the thought. I'm not going to be here tomorrow when they come. I can't listen to the axes and chainsaws." I turned and ran upstairs, slammed my door and dropped onto my bed. Resting my chin on my hands, I stared out my window until my eyes watered and sleep came over me. It was my final view of my majestic, magical, miraculous maple, and I wanted it to last forever.

I woke the following morning to the clatter and clumsy clanging of men with tools. My heart pounded, I felt sick and nauseous, but I foolishly willed myself to look toward my window. Turning my head slowly to the right and peeking between my fingers like a kid at a horror film, I exhaled at the sight of two tiny orange leaves flapping playfully in the wind.

Furiously, I ran to the window, opened it and climbed right out onto that gentle limb. Still in my nightgown, dew covering the bark, I shimmied myself across and up then tried to find a comfortable position to lie alongside her body. Skin to bark, I rested my cheek tenderly upon her. I patted her and whispered, "I'm sorry I let you down. I love you."

Tears mixed with dew, I closed my eyes. Instinctively, I

began humming our song, hmmm, hmmm, hmm, hmm, turn, turn. Our song, "Turn, Turn, Turn", what else could it be. The Byrds released their version just a few days before I was born. My dad remembers it playing on the radio when he drove my mom to the labor ward.

As they returned home and pulled into the driveway with their new baby girl, he heard it again. He found himself humming to it. Then he noticed the maple. He says (now I have to take his word here) that he turned to me and whispered, "That's your song, Maclyn, yours and your maple".

Motors revving jolted me out of my memory. I looked down and saw Tim's guys. I think I heard one say "There's a kid up there".

I scooted back, gently lifting my leg over her limb and pulled myself onto my knees. I edged my way back to my room and climbed inside. Before closing the sash, I leaned out and grabbed those last two dancing orange leaves. I kissed her limb and closed the window.

I pulled my curtains shut, quickly dressed, ran downstairs and out the door over to Paisley's. She stood out front waiting for me.

"Bet you didn't have breakfast yet," she ventured as she uncharacteristically offered her arm around me and brought me inside.

I didn't say a word.

While Paisley and I silently shoveled some sort of breakfast cereal into our mouths in her back den, staring out at her pool, I thought about my grandpa. He sort of popped into my mind. He was in the hospital still at this point, and I wondered what he would say about the chopping down of his granddaughter's best friend.

I wondered what he thought about my song, about its anti-war theme and the fight I lost against saving my first best friend. I took another bite of cereal. I think I knew what he might say.

He might say there is a time for everything and a purpose. I think I would have to agree.

6

DREAMING MY FUTURE

My last visit to the cancer ward where Grandpa lived in a dreary private room next door to other dying patients comprised me, Mom and Grandma. Grandma practically lived there. The hospital staff, used to family hanging on like this, even set up a cot near Grandpa, telling Grandma she could stay anytime. So she did, often.

When Grandpa entered the hospital September 1977, and the doctors said he might be there for quite a while (never saying anything about him dying there), Mom and Dad helped Grandma sell her house and move into a small apartment two and a half blocks from the hospital. That way she could walk over any time she wanted. I think Grandma knew what was coming.

I wish I had known when I was there for my last visit, that I had known it was my last visit, because then I could have told Grandpa things, or asked him things, or well … maybe it wouldn't've made any difference at all if I had known. What would I have said anyway? What do you say to someone who's about to die?

Grandpa called it "dreaming your future". He said that's

how you develop intelligently, with purpose, not chance or luck. So I dream my future, fantasize, drift off into the world when I'm an adult and imagine. It's hard to stay there, in the future. I think it helps me to know more about my past. Somehow, past and future seem connected. It's the past that defines the future, but the future shapes you each moment. Grandpa could explain this better.

He always knew how to make simple things seem extraordinary. Mom had a pretty cool dad.

I never met my dad's parents. So it's strange to think of them as part of my future, too; but they are. Kenny and Eric met them when they were just babies, so they don't remember much. Mom and Dad married right out of college and had Kenny a few years later.

My parents are in their forties now. Dad's parents were 50 when they died. I bet Dad thinks about that sometimes, wondering if he will surpass them.

Grandma and Grandpa Mills lived, married, and almost died in England. In the 1940s, Grandpa Mills' bond company transferred him to their new offices in California right in the midst of World War II. The company had ties to Hollywood and wanted to get out of the conflict. After the London Blitz, the boss pretty much packed up his company's bags and fled the country. For my grandparents, it was a chance for them to see part of the world, and America represented growth and hope. Plus, the office was in West Hollywood, and you can't get more American than that.

Dad was just seven years old when they moved here. With three kids under ten, the move couldn't have been easy, though. A mere 15 years later, after watching Eric and Kenny perform as snowflakes in a winter preschool production in Santa Nina, my grandparents were killed driving along the slippery lanes of the I-10 near Pasadena.

On his bedroom bureau, Dad keeps an old black and

white photo of Grandma and Grandpa Mills leaning against a white picket fence at his childhood home in England. Dad doesn't talk much about them now.

In fact, the only member of his family he talks about at all is his older sister, Aunt Sue. She was two when they moved here. I like her a lot.

I don't have many relatives. Grandma, Uncle Bert, and there's Dad's older brother Frank who I'm not sure even exists. Supposedly, he's a bit older than Dad and lives back in London. None of us, not even Mom, have ever met him. Neither he nor Dad ever phone or write one another. I know absolutely nothing else about him, not even what he does for a living.

I'm sure it's something really cool, like mob work or secret agent government stuff, because whenever I bring it up, Dad changes the subject. Aunt Sue agrees. She hardly hears from him either.

Once in a while, she tells us that Frank is well, or that he's just out of the hospital for a broken foot or something. We usually only see Aunt Sue once a year when she and Uncle Henry drive down from Portland to see "all of these handsome nephews and such a lovely niece." They don't have any children.

As far as I know, neither does Uncle Frank. Neither does Mom's brother. Well, Uncle Bert had an adopted son once. In a way, I suppose it's a good thing that I have these four brothers, being that I don't have any cousins (not anymore). Since Uncle Bert moved across the country, we had hardly seen him until Grandpa got sick.

When I think of all that Grandma's been through in her life, I'm guessing this is just one more for the books. She's pretty tough. When she was near my age, 12, her parents gave her up. It was 1916, just before the start of the Russian Revolution. They had sent her to France. Grandpa's parents died when he was 15, and Grandma doesn't really know what exactly happened to hers.

At the time, Grandpa Ben and his twin sister, Hannah, were smuggled out of Russia by relatives. Grandpa would always try to recall his parents. He didn't think the soldiers got both of them. He liked to tell the story of his father jumping in the way of gunfire to save his wife.

Grandpa was an old romantic. I just love that about him. I want to be in love some day. I do. I want to experience love, the good stuff. Mostly, I want to feel that first kiss. But I don't want to talk about that stuff yet.

Back to Grandpa and Great-Aunt Hannah.

They made it to France and found an orphanage. Even though they were teenagers, they figured an orphanage would help them get on their feet. That's where Grandpa Ben met Grandma Millie, who had been there since the nuns had found her wrapped in a black dress on their doorsteps. No records could ever be found on her so she's always had to guess at her age.

When they figured she was 18, they let her leave the orphanage. They judged her age with Grandpa Ben's and Hannah's. Ben and Millie were pretty much in love by then, so the three of them took on some odd jobs and eventually gathered enough money together to sail for New York.

Just months after they arrived, in May 1923, Ben and Millie married. A few years later, they moved to California where Grandpa Ben started work in the building industry. Soon after, Uncle Bert arrived in the world, born on American soil, the first generation of Lancere's here.

So my mother's side - part Russian, a little French. Or, as Grandpa Ben used to say: "French surname, Russian souls, like the famous sculptor who carries our name, Eugene Lancere."

Somewhere after Uncle Bert and before Mom, Grandma Millie had another baby, but she died at two. I don't think

Mom was actually planned. She's a lot younger than her big brother Bert. Just like my brothers and me. There's something strange, though, about her birth.

Grandpa loved telling stories about how he thought Mom was the baby (Winnie) who had died, and then she came back as herself (named Francine). It was weird to hear him talk about it.

He told us once, "Your mother, Francine, used to talk about Uncle Bert's little blue necktie with a yellow sailboat on it. He wore it to his first day of school when he was six. The funny thing was, your mom wasn't born yet. We don't even have any of Bert's first day of school pictures. In fact, he lost the tie the next year after baby Winnie died. So, our Francine came to us with Winnie inside her."

"Nonsense," Mom says.

"I think he's onto something," says Dad. "Your mom is psychic."

"Well, you're a bit psycho," she jokes back.

Whatever it is, it's weird. Eric says Mom inherited the baby's soul. I don't know what to think. I would like to think, though, that someone in my family has psychic powers. That'd be so cool.

The only time I can read anyone's mind is when I haven't done my Saturday morning chores by lunchtime, and I know Dad's going to come in my room and tell me I can't go to the movies with Marc and Kevin until they're done. (My brothers used to take me nearly every weekend because I was half-price, $1; but now that I'm 13, they say I have to pay my own way. Seems their love isn't as deep as their pockets.)

At six-foot-three, Dad can be intimidating. Really, though, he's just a big gentle bear. Mom thinks so, too.

He's never hit any of my brothers or me. Ever. If he's angry, he just stands there and says loudly, "Maclyn, you are not going to the movies today. You are going outside to finish sweeping the patio. Now."

Then he smiles, bends all six-feet-three of himself down and kisses the top of my head, and he walks out of my room.

If dreaming your future really works, then I dream a future of gentle bears to surround me and protect me. Hey, it's working. That's what I've got right now with all these big brothers.

7

NOT JUST ONE OF THE BOYS

Grandpa had so many good ideas. He collected a lot of wisdom in his lifetime. Just like my maple. I can't seem to get over the loss of both of these beings in such a short time. And I can't shake those last days at the hospital with Grandpa.

Somehow, death carries a smell. You can sense it's on its way. Maybe not exactly when, but you can smell it getting closer. That's how I remember it now.

Saturday, November 25, 1978, age 13, the hospital

Mom took Grandma down to the cafeteria for a meal a few minutes after we'd arrived, so I sat alone with my grandfather, secretly fearing he would die right there with just the two of us. The thought of running down to the café to tell Mom and Grandma was too much to bear.

Fortunately, this grim deed never materialized. In fact, Grandpa seemed stronger than usual that day. Probably because we'd caught him before his medicine, so he wasn't drowsy. Still, pastiness marked his face. A pale, hospital gown whiteness spread across his wrinkled skin, and tubes traveled in and around his whole body: two entered his nostrils, pumping in small jets of oxygen; one pierced his left hand, trailing up to a yellowy looking bag hung from a metal hook; another wrapped around his forearm, dripping in a clearer substance; and a final tube splintered into several tentacles each patched to different sections of his chest, carrying no liquids, just providing a quiet rhythm for that bleeping TV-like machine.

Grandpa lay still, only moving his eyes across my face, then out toward the window, then back to me. I held his free tubeless right hand. With restricted movements, confined to tubes of plastic, I often served as a toe-scratcher, water-getter, blanket-puller-upper or just hand-holder (my favorite task). Grandpa never complained. He'd just smile, say something about God needing good help, gently squeeze my hand, and occasionally nod off.

Seeing someone at his weakest, especially someone I loved, stirred up a resistance in me, a gurgle in my chest that pushed its way toward my throat, threatening to scream out, "This isn't fair!" So I sat silently remembering this man, so tall, gentle yet critical.

Each time we visited, he seemed to shrink, having shrunk nearly a foot within the last year; and he appeared smaller again as he lay motionless in that hospital bed - pale, thin. Helpless. When he spoke with that once deep voice – so deep that it often frightened me – nothing more than a whisper escaped passed his pencil-thin lips. A very throaty whisper. His sunken cheeks bellowed in, then out, in, out, like a tired bagpipe. After every few words, he'd have to take a deep breath. Then he'd continue, sometimes with his watery brown eyes open, sometimes closed; but always, I would sit right next to him, so he could place his old wrinkled hand on mine.

Once in a while the hand would squeeze my tiny fingers, seemingly independent of real intention, perhaps due to a spasm, a sudden reaching out, kind of like when you're falling asleep and feel like you're actually falling, you jerk, afraid you're going to hit ground. Usually, he'd ask about school or my poetry. He always wanted to hear a poem, and he'd never mind if I'd read one he'd all ready heard.

He told me each time, "Lovely, Maclyn dear, just lovely. You are a poet. A true poet." However, this time, since Mom and Grandma weren't there, since we filled the room just the two of us, just me and my dying grandfather, we didn't speak about school or poetry or how he felt. This time, we talked about more important things.

Grandpa, perhaps sensing the imminence of his death, chose to really speak to me.

*   *   *

Sometimes when you are remembering things that carry so much emotion, you need to stop. Remembering Grandpa brings up lots of feelings. I don't exactly know what to do with them. Mom says girls are emotional. She says that makes us good moms because we care so much.

My brothers and Dad, they don't ever cry. They aren't girls. That's for sure. I wonder what they really think of me, being this girl with all these feelings. I wonder if they wish I were a boy, like Dad does.

Dad likes to call me Mac (like one of the boys), which is actually one of the reasons I wanted to change it. I think he wanted all boys; because if you think about it, he wanted to name me Jacqueline, which can be shortened to Jack. Then he named me Maclyn, which he always shortens to Mac. Five sons would make a basketball team. Four sons and one daughter make a sorry father.

For example, what do little girls usually receive for their seventh birthdays? A doll maybe? Or a new dress? Or a tea set? How about a tiny tot's baseball set, inclusive of a bat, mitt, ball and an application for little league? I never was big on dolls to begin with (did I even have the chance?), but I think at that age I'd have rather had tea parties with my teddy bear than sit in the dirt with smelly seven-year-old boys whose daily highlights were to see who could kill the most ants with torpedoing spit.

Besides, seven-year-old girls can be very insecure about their femininity. During baseball season, Mom helped out a little. She'd tie a nice pink bow on my head before our games, even bought me a pretty satin one when my team made it to little league finals (not by any help of my athletic talents).

I certainly wasn't the star of the team, and no one called me Little Miss Slugger. I was lucky if I got up to bat once during an entire game. The only reason for me being on the team at all was probably because Dad worked with Coach Phillips. Despite my freak appearances in the batter's box or out in Left Field (my assigned position, and you know what that means), the whole family never failed to show up, just to get a glimpse of the batter with the pink bow.

Thank goodness that only lasted two years. I played for the Apaches and the Braves. Had I stuck it out another year, I could have been an Indian or a Chief.

By age nine, I had decided my place in Life was not sitting in a smelly dugout with little league boys who told dirty jokes, bad dirty jokes at that. So for my ninth birthday, Mom bought me a set of Nancy Drew mystery books. Thus began my short yet adventurous career as a detective.

That ambition ended before I turned ten and had gotten myself locked in the attic for eight hours, because "I thought I heard something up there". Turned out, what I'd heard was our neighbor's cat lurking about. Still, one good thing did come from that little exploit, but it wasn't finding the Gold's cat (which believe me is so ugly we were all better off with it missing). I found the hole in the chimneystack and the reason why the house filled up with smoke whenever we'd build a fire.

Because I found the hole and because Mom and Dad were so relieved I hadn't run away or been kidnapped, I wasn't scolded. But you'd better believe that was the last set of

Nancy Drew mysteries I ever received.

I am happy to be *amongst* the boys. I just want it to be clear to everyone that I am not one *of* the boys.

8

THAT INVISIBLE WHISPER
(AND A FEW TEARS)

"How's my ... lovely girl?" Grandpa asked between breaths, between his few remaining breaths. Squeezing my hand, he pushed his thin lips up into a half-smile. This moment marked my final visit with Grandpa. Something I didn't realize at the time. That's why I want to keep remembering everything now, so I never forget later.

"Fine, Grandpa. I'm good." I squeezed back as he tried to smile again then closed his eyes. "You know my friend, Paisley, Grandpa?"

"Paisley Grandpa ... don't know ... her," he smiled.

"Grandpa, you're silly," I teased. "Paisley, you know, my neighbor? Well, we have this kind of group, and-"

His eyes opened wide as he gazed up at me, waiting. Sometimes his look shot straight through me as if he knew every thought I was thinking. As if he knew how often I thought about Joe Basketball and what I wanted to do with him and how I felt so much dumber than Paisley and how secretly I wished she'd fail something so that I could be the smarter friend.

Then, as if to purposefully interrupt my daydreams, he whispered, "Maclyn. I want to ... tell ... you something ... something very ... important. You must listen ... listen carefully. You know ... little girl ... you know ... I'm dying ... I'm going to die ... soon, very soon. You must ... know that." I nodded, squeezed his hand lightly then tighter, trying uselessly to hold back tears brought on by his sudden tenderness.

"Are you scared, Grandpa?"

"No," he said, and I believed him. Then, with less assurance, "No, I don't ... think so. Not yet." He licked his dry lips and swallowed. I reached for some ice chips, feeding him a few, letting his tongue lick them in while his lips purposefully pulled them inside his mouth. "I want to ... tell you, Maclyn ... some things. I never talked ... with you. Not like with ... Kenny, and the ... boys. I want to ... I want you ... to be prepared. You must love ... must learn to love ... Life. Maclyn, you must make a ... Life that you ... love. Love your Life. Understand?"

I looked at him - his tired face, the heavy bags under his watery eyes, the dried and wrinkling skin that covered his lived-in face like millions of tiny riverbeds. The thinning white hair, and his red lips so out of place like a daisy in the desert; they were the only feature that gave his fragile face any life at all. Even his big brown eyes that never stopped tearing looked lost to Time's wicked thieving hands.

*   *   *

Let me stop for a moment, catch my breath. Eric meditates when he needs to get it together. I've been thinking a lot about that lately. As I'm newly 13, I've been thinking a lot about religion. I've always wondered about God, Goddess, All That Is, but I've never really completely got it. I listen to my intuition, and I know that something is there with me, but I guess I'm just waiting for a bigger sign than a silent voice. Eric says the silence *is* the bigger sign. That's why he meditates.

My family has never claimed to be part of any religion. When I ask my parents, my mom says she thinks her people were probably Russian Jews, but her parents never raised her Jewish. They always said grace at dinner, and often told Mom to pray for different people who got sick. They even went to church, but they never said, "Well, we're -, so you should do - or not do - because -." You know, Ben and Millie just tried to raise good kids.

Dad's the same. His parents were probably Protestants, he thinks. But he never remembers going to church. And when his family moved out to California, to Hollywood, he just remembers his dad working, his mom helping the kids with homework, and the family swimming on weekends.

Never much talk of God or anything. I look at my dad and think, *Well, he turned out pretty good. He's a pretty nice guy, so what's the point of all this religion stuff anyway?*

My parents tell us, "You'll figure it all out. You make the choices. We're not going to tell you what to choose. Just be nice."

Dad always tells my brothers, "Character builds the man. That's what's important. What you take away from your experiences - whether they were good for you or not - is character. And character is always a good thing."

Well, yeah, I guess; but sometimes Dad goes a bit far with his character building theory. Several years ago when I was just a tree-climbing 8-year-old, Dad took Marc and me to a Lakers' game. At the intermission, Marc walked me to the concession stand for some cokes. Marc's the youngest brother, just three years my senior. As we climbed back up the stands, I tripped and dumped the coke all over myself.

Spring 1974, age eight, Lakers' game

"Mac!" Dad whispered loudly, "What in the world have you done? Go on, get up. Weren't you paying attention? Oh, for – look at you, you're a mess. Now, go on, clean yourself off."

"But Dad, I jus-"

"Don't cry now. Just get up and go clean yourself off. I don't want you all sticky. Stop cryin'."

I felt everyone's eyes staring right through me, but I couldn't look up. Why was he so upset? Why couldn't I cry? Marc just looked my way, as if to say, *I'm sorry, Mac, I can't help you. You just gotta be a man like Dad.*

He stood there, hands in his pockets, head bowed.

"I'm sorry, Dad," I said as I picked myself up and streams of sticky brown fluid rolled down my pink T-shirt, off my jeans and onto the floor, forming another sticky mess around my new white Keds. "I don't know what happened. I was watching where ..." I couldn't quite put my words together. Salty tears blurred my vision so that I couldn't see Dad or Marc. A fire burned inside me.

"There's no need for apologies. Now, quit cryin'. Don't be such a girl. If that were Marc, he wouldn't still be standing there, and he sure as heck wouldn't be cryin'." He shook his head, sat down and turned to my brother. "Marc, take your sister to the bathroom. None of this cryin' business, Maclyn."

The burning turned to stinging. My name rang loudly in my head. *Maclyn.* He called me Maclyn, my full name, the one written in ink on that same birth certificate that declared me "female". Was he reminding me that I was indeed the little girl, one among many boys, the one mistake of the crew? Why couldn't he simply acknowledge that yes, this was his little girl, and she deserved this moment to show her emotions?

I practically ran to the toilets, forcing Marc to employ his deflecting football techniques, dodging patrons with their own teetering sodas, trying to keep up with me. Once inside, half-blinded by my tears, I wanted to flush myself down one of those blue-water bowls. I cowered inside that white-tiled, antiseptically cold, porcelain room until the game's final two minutes. Marc stood outside, never saying a word to me.

For a long time after, I truly wished I'd never come out.

I couldn't believe Dad's lecture on my crying. Stinging seeds of anger bubbled in my belly, leaving no room for embarrassment. Room for hurt, yes. His shouts echoed. Tears. That's all, I thought, they were just silly wet drops of saltwater.

It wasn't until two days later that I recalled the fall. The reason for the tears. I had hurt myself. Stepping out of the shower, I noticed a larger yellow bruise on my right thigh - the baby stroller. The mother had set it on the stairs, leaving little room for passersby. I had tripped over a baby stroller.

Anyway, the next time I cried in front of Dad was last October. For a while after the Laker game, I'd just shimmy up my maple for privacy. Tissues in my front pocket, self-pity in my back. Something I loved about that tree: It never pitied me, absorbing my tears within its hard bark. No evidence of my sorrow left behind.

These days, if I need to cry, it's usually by myself.

Maybe when Mom gets home, we can talk about crying and stuff. I don't hold much hope, though. To be honest, Mom and I just don't talk about that kind of stuff. I love her and she loves me, but it's more a mother/daughter relationship than a Mom/Maclyn relationship - if you know what I mean. We share news but not secrets. We share thoughts but not feelings. I don't even know if Mom believes in God.

Isn't that something a kid should know about her Mom? Dad always says things like, "God'll take care of that" or "God only knows". So he's got some kind of relationship going on up there. Mom, though, I can't be sure.

Perhaps for some people, that connection to something greater than us can only be experienced at the end of our life instead of throughout it. For me, something greater existed inside my maple. She was my connection - something Grandpa understood.

But it wasn't until his last day at the hospital when I realized he had always listened to me talk about my real best friend. Grandpa shared something that simply rocked my world.

9

GRANDPA'S WORDS

In that cold hospital room, what would become the final moments before Grandpa died, I simply stared at him as he spoke to me. I listened better than I'd ever done before. His words carried thoughts I wanted to savor.

Desperately trying not to wander off in typical Eliza-daydream style, I fixed my attention on the speaker until the speaker spoke no more.

November 25, 1978, age 13, the hospital room

"Grandpa, I don't understand," I admitted, eager for his wisdom while simultaneously aware of the breath each word took - guilty, again, for wanting to know, but afraid of what my wanting was taking from him.

"You must not ... give up ... on Life. Never give ... up. God is ... always there ... waiting ... waiting for you ... waiting with you. You must learn ... learn to trust, to trust God. Even when it ... seems ... that He is being ... cruel. He is not. You must ... be patient. Love. Love yourself. Believe ... in you. That is the ... the only way ... for God to be ... be with you ... in you."

My mind scrambled to understand, trying purposefully to separate my own ideas from what he was telling me, trying to stop my own babble, "Goddess, God, Goddess". Trying to focus on the nuggets, the whole, the point.

"Okay, Grandpa, I see. I think. But why is He taking you now, like this, with so much pain? Why can't we just tell God that we've got it all under control here. You can live with us."

"No ... we need to ... we can't ... interfere. He needs me ... now. He needs ... my soul. My soul ... it has ... other jobs. Like your ... tree. We have other ... work. I have lived ... seventy ... seventy-six years. But now ... because God wills it ... I have ... I am ill. It's okay ... I'm ready. But I want to ... tell you ... these things, before..." he stopped, licked his lips, swallowed.

He motioned for more ice chips. Again his lips pulled in the tiny fragments while his tongue savored the coolness. He sucked on them for a few moments then swallowed, closed his eyes, and I thought that was it. He was gone, gone before he told me, told me what might matter most of all. But then I saw his eyes flicker. He was just resting. I breathed; unaware I was holding my breath.

I looked around the empty white room as I'd done so often the past year. A few plants adorned the small white wooden shelf in the corner, a color TV rudely protruded from the wall, and a photograph of Grandma, Aunt Hannah, Mom, and Bert rested next to a clean bedpan on his bedside table.

The only other accessories in the bland room, save two metal chairs, were two clear plastic sacks that hung wearily from shiny metal poles on either side of his bed. They stood like a pair of reliable sentries guarding a general. They reminded me of something. I watched them drip in time to the TV-machines' bleeping, in tune with Grandma's traveling alarm clock, joining together harmoniously in a morbid death march of Time.

My thoughtful gaze soon returned to my ailing grandfather met equally by this gentle man's penetrating eyes. He managed a smile. "I can see ... little girl ... you do not ... understand ... why God ... does this. No one truly ... understands. But if we ... trust ... in ... in ourselves ... then we do not need ... to understand. It is given."

I struggled to keep up with his words, his thoughts. My maple came to mind. "How can we just believe in someone who we don't see? How can we just trust someone like that, Grandpa? Sometimes, you know, I don't even trust Mom or Dad, so how am I supposed to trust God?"

"We don't know ... who ... or what ... is God. Truly know. But ... we do know ... we know that – " he paused, patted my hands. "Do you ever ... dear Maclyn ... do you ever ... have a feeling ... about something? Just a ... feeling ... that something is right ... or wrong? Like knowing ... that you should be ... nice, polite ... to people? Knowing it is ... wrong to say rude ... things ... to them? Do you ever ... ever just feel ... that?"

"Sometimes. Yeah. Sometimes I have instincts that tell me I shouldn't say certain things to Paisley because it might be mean. I get jealous of her because she's so smart. I think I know what you're saying. Pais says it's intuition, that that is God, or, uh, Goddess."

"Yes, for her. But ... do you believe ... that ... for yourself? Truly?"

"Well, Pais says –"

"No, not ... Paisley. Maclyn," Grandpa interrupted then quieted. He looked up at me, gripping my hand tighter. I looked down, suddenly realizing it was me grasping his hand. "Little girl ... you mustn't ... mustn't always ... listen to ... your friends. You must ask ... yourself ... what you think. Understand?"

"Yes, Grandpa. But I trust Paisley. And sometimes she knows a lot. You know Mom, Grandpa, Mom doesn't always have time -"

He interrupted again, but this time he didn't seem upset. "Sweet Maclyn ... mothers are busy ... people. You can't ... rely on her ... either. No more than ... on your little ... neighbor. Listen. Trust Maclyn. What does ... Maclyn think?

Ask her. Not Mother ... not Father ... not Paisley. You can ... ask ... them, but, ask ... Maclyn, too. She knows ... knows what's best ... for you. Learn to ... trust. Believe." He closed his eyes, relaxed his head against his pillow. "I remember ... a little girl ... a sweet little girl ... who used to ... climb a majestic ... tree. She loved ... the tree ... and she knew ... the tree ... loved her. She believed."

The grip on my hands loosened. Mine. His. Again the room fell silent but for the dripping and ticking and beating. And soon Grandpa's weak breaths joined the morbid choir of machines.

Some days, a moment meets you like a ton of bricks. This was one of them. I could feel its importance, but I couldn't grasp its entirety. I knew his words needed to marinate inside me, stew until I understood. These were words to ponder not act on.

And so, I pondered.

10

POSSIBILITIES YET UNSEEN

Life sometimes skips from one confusing moment to another. A tree one day stands tall and proud, the next day it's gone forever. A grandfather tickles you and calls you "the bee's knees". Suddenly, he's frail in a bed, dying, then gone. Life is change. There's no stopping it. Life moves toward its own known conclusion seemingly carrying us along as passengers.

A week after Grandpa died, Mom flew with Grandma to New York. She settled her in with Uncle Bert then flew back to be with us for Christmas.

The night Dad was set to drive Mom back to the airport for her second trip to New York, I overheard them talking in their bedroom. Drawers opened and closed, closets slid back and forth. Occasionally, silence. Then sobbing. Then "Shh, it's okay, Honey." Then more drawers.

"Now, Francine, it's all right. You know he's out of pain. He's resting, he's out of pain. He was ready to go. Be thankful he didn't have to suffer any longer."

The crying stopped briefly, replaced by sniffles.

"I know. I just hope the kids didn't realize how painful it was for him." Mom's hurt filled my own heart. "He always tried so hard to make them believe he was okay. And Maclyn would sit there and hold his hand, and Marc would make him laugh. He really liked that. I just wish Eric had visited more often."

I listened silently, trying to hold back my own tears.

"Don't worry, Honey. You need to think about your trip now, taking care of your mother. She'll need you. We'll be fine."

"Yes, I know. Everything will be okay. Soon. I know."

It took everything not to just rush in and hug her, to tell her I knew, and that it was okay, that I loved my grandpa, that I missed him, but that it was okay. I wanted to share what he had said to me, about my maple, about believing, but now didn't seem quite the right time.

Mom returned home after a few days then flew back to New York after Christmas. It's been about a week. I can't wait until she's home for good. I want to tell her about Grandpa and how he's probably climbing my maple right now.

Funny how it doesn't seem natural to just go up and hug my mom, out of the blue. (Eric's the family member for hugs.) I love my mom, but she probably spends more time on herself than us. She's what many people would call "naturally beautiful". I wonder then why she spends so much time in front of the mirror ensuring her youthful looks. Youthful good looks she tells me that I will one day be thankful for.

I wouldn't mind being as pretty as Mom when I grow up. Some people say we look alike now. I don't think so. People just say that to be kind, thinking I might worry that I resemble my seventy-percent male family. After all, girls are supposed to look like their mothers and boys their fathers. Well, this just isn't so in our family.

Eric looks a lot like Mom; except that he's about half a foot taller than her 5' 5" frame. The three of us – me, Mom, Eric – have similar features: thick, dark brown hair, deep, dark brown eyes, and round, freckle-free faces. Right now,

Mom and I are the same height. I sure hope to sprout another inch or so, though. She and I stand in the giant shadows of all the Mills' men. Dad and my brothers are each at least 6 feet. And Marc is only 16.

I guess the boys take after Dad's height. Lucky for them. And all of them, except Eric, have Dad's light brown hair. Somehow, Kenny, my oldest brother, inherited the Mills' recessive redhead gene. At 21, Kenny is Dad's spitting image (minus the red hair). Tall, skinny, compassionate brown eyes, warm hands, and a corny sense of humor.

Paisley could even fit into our family picture. Her wavy auburn hair, dark brown eyes and freckled nose complete her natural beauty. Pais is beautiful in the way I imagine Mom was as a little girl - before she discovered the make-up counter.

Linda's Irish, so that's probably where Paisley gets her naturally healthy good looks. But her nose is definitely her dad's - pure Romanesque, straight, pointed and confident. Pais is a little shorter than me - about 5' 3" - but she'll most likely end up being 5' 6" or so. With Linda taller than my mom but Bob shorter than my dad, I imagine that Pais and I will even out.

Genes are funny, you know; just when you think you've studied everyone in the family and you have a rough idea how you'll end up, in pops some funny trait no one ever likes to talk about. This is the excuse my dad uses for my disobedience.

"It's my brother Frank's fault. He was a sneaky one, that Frank."

I don't go for the genetic family stuff, the past. I think it's my future that defines me. It's who I will be that shapes who I am now, like a lump of clay spinning on a potter's wheel, manipulated by skilled hands into a curvaceous urn resembling not so much Grecian artifacts but more modern designs. Gently influenced by ancient forms while desiring change, and taking shape into new patterns only imagined in the artist's mind.

That is the shape of me, an idea of what is to come, sculpted by craftsmen's hands of a recent past. Thoughts like these excite me about the future.

They are the possibilities yet unseen.

11

THE ARMY TENT INCIDENT

It's true, if we could see into our future, we might relax. Grandpa says to believe, to trust. I'm workin' on it.

I suppose if anyone's keeping a scorecard on the times I trust my instincts and things work out and the times I fail miserably, it'd be an even count. I'm working on the whole growing up thing, but it just doesn't seem to be getting easier. Especially the boy part.

Sure, I noticed the whole changing thing years ago - about four or five years ago. Boys and girls are different. Maybe it took me longer because I'd grown up in a household of brothers and that's just how they treated me – as just one more guy.

But as my body changed, and their bodies changed, well, let's just say that with four older brothers there's a lot to notice.

At what point did my brothers' friends appear as more than distant cousins? To them, I'm "little Mac," so-and-so's kid sister. No one's aware of my daydream stares as Marc's pal Eddie glides through our kitchen in his ripped Levi's and navy blue polo shirt whose right collar curls up from so many washings. Unbeknownst to him, he possesses the power to melt my knees and disconnect my brain cords that operate my speech.

Paisley laughs at my ogling. "Oh, Eliza," she says in her ladies' club voice, "don't let these guys fool you. Don't let them take your mind off more important matters, like the organization or the Goddess. You're not forgetting about these things, are you? They do this on purpose, you know. Boys!" (Picture that one syllable with a tight-lipped humph! and a quick turn of the head to the right.) "They try to distract you from these things. Don't let them..." And away she rants for at least another 20 minutes. I'll spare you.

Distracted? Me? By boys? Hmmm. Okay, maybe a little.

But what's more important than Eddie Hall's blue eyes, or the way he seems to blush when he passes me, barely saying "hi", but saying it with such shyness that I want to accidentally let my arm brush his, so that maybe if we touch, he'll feel just that bit closer to me, and say more than a quiet "hi", he'll say my name, "Hi, Eliza".

Or how about rosy-cheeked Joe Basketball in third period English? (Have I told you about my crush on Joe?) Just thinking about him reading Robert Frost's "Stopping by Woods" sends chills straight up my teen-aged spine.

I've had my first kiss. *Technically*. A peck on the lips from Steven Wood on the jungle gym in first grade; he ran off and didn't say another word to me until the third grade when he called me a Tom Boy for climbing the school's rotting oak tree. Boys can be so fickle.

I just want to fall in love. *Sigh*. That phrase – 'falling in love'. I want to explore, window shop at Life's tree of forbidden knowledge, sample the wares but not buy anything.

Actually, I've done my share of sampling. I remember the first time I saw "something". One might think a girl with four brothers prancing around the house must have caught an innocent glimpse at the male anatomy several times already. Not that it never occurred to me to look. After all, they are my brothers. It's just that Mom strictly enforces a dress code at all times. Bathrobes are recommended, but towels are accepted.

The first time I saw what hid behind those towels was in the fifth grade.

For a ten-year-old girl, spring signifies nothing more than extra daylight to play in, Easter vacation, and, of course, the ice cream man. So when my across-the-street neighbor, 12-year-old Billy Gold, asked me if I wanted to play guessing games in his homemade tent that spring of 1976, who was I to question his seemingly good neighbor intentions?

My memory's blurred so much of what happened, but I think I can paint a near-vivid picture. I remember it was a sunny Saturday and I was on my way next door to visit Paisley for lunch. I was wearing my cut-off shorts and Kenny's old Rolling Stones T-shirt.

Spring 1976, age ten, the Gold's backyard

"Heyya Maclyn, what's up?" Billy leapt out from behind our Juniper bush like a bad dream. Sporting his typical uniform of faded jeans and a black Kiss T-shirt, Billy was something that showed up every now and again to disturb your quiet thoughts.

"Hey, yourself," I shot back. "I don't like being scared like that, Billy. What're you doing crawling around behind there, anyway? If you're looking for Marc or Kevin, they're at a game."

Although Billy was a neighbor and nearly the same age as Marc, no friendship had ever formed between him and my brothers. Unfortunately, that never stopped him from coming by to show them his new baseball glove or skateboard. The Gold's moved away this past August. Mr. Gold was in banking (I love that, perfect job for someone named Gold). I think their move had something to do with all the "great new gifts" Billy got that everyone *had* to see.

"Oh, that's too bad," Billy said, "because I've just built this cool new tent in my yard. I slept in it last night. It's totally awesome. Too bad Marc or Kevin aren't here." *Awkward pause.* "Hey, I know, maybe you want to see it. Huh, Mac?" I hesitated a bit but thought the tent sounded neat. Billy's new toys never much interested me, but I'd never been inside a tent before. It sounded fun. Paisley's peanut butter sandwiches could wait.

"Okay, just for a minute."

We crossed the street and entered through the wooden gate into the Gold's compact backyard. The seven-foot square army tent nearly filled it. Following behind Billy, I squeezed past some prickly bushes and crawled underneath a dying lemon tree before reaching the tent's front flap.

Alas, inside, nothing more than I had expected - just the basic insides of one green army tent. Shady, completely bare but for a blue nylon sleeping bag and pillow in the left corner, a red flashlight and an empty packet of Oreo cookies.

"Uh, it's neat," I half-muttered, wondering about all the excitement to see this tent. I remembered Paisley. "Well, the tent's cool, but I told Paisley I'd be over at noon and it's almost quarter past now. So, uh, I'd better go."

"No, wait!" Frantically, he grabbed my arm, leaving me with an Indian burn as I tried to escape his grip.

"C'mon, Billy, I said I was going, now quit it!"

"Okay, but first," he glanced quickly about his tent, then flashed the broad Billy Gold smile and said, "First, do you want to see something else? Something better?"

Billy's infamous shifty grin spread even wider across his redheaded pale face, and I knew he had something he wasn't supposed to have or something that would scare me, like the snake he'd found in the gutter last summer. I figured that whatever it was this time couldn't be as bad as that slimy snake. He got such a good laugh out of scaring me with it that I vowed never to let him the satisfaction of frightening me again. Besides, whatever it was, I could always get Marc or Kevin to beat him up. Settled.

"Okay, Billy, what is it?"

He secured the flap and motioned me to stand next to his sleeping bag. "You have four older brothers, right?" I nodded impatiently, easily looking bored. "Well, have you ever seen them? You know, really seen them?" I gave him that squinty-eyed, cocked head look, the universal sign that says, "What are you talking about?"

"Well, I've got a little deal for you. Sort of a game, see. I'll show you mine if you show me yours."

"Mine? Mine what?"

"You know. Your ... thing." And he waved a pointed finger somewhere around my belly area. I looked down. What was there, I thought, that he wanted to see...? Oh, my god! He wanted to see me! I was just about ready to run out of the tent when I thought, *It's only show and tell.* That's innocent, harmless. Isn't it?

I thought for an instant about God. What would He think? And the Goddess? She couldn't be too happy about my next move, but I was ten and incredibly curious. Why not?

"Okay then. You go first," I said, hands on hips, trying to look as calm and uninterested as possible.

I thought I glimpsed a moment of shock on his face, but then quickly (probably trying to move on before I changed my mind) he undid his button, stood up, pulled down his zipper then just dropped them. His pants fell around his knees, underwear crumpled above them. Billy Gold stood before me, arms folded. I wasn't quite sure where to look, and found I couldn't help but stare at him, at his, at, well, you know. It was just there, hanging, looking at me, saying, See, this is a boy.

Was I supposed to be impressed? I was, I think, actually a bit disappointed, and slightly grossed out. It was just so, so fleshy.

"Well, whaddya think? Something, isn't it?"

I envisioned dissatisfied moviegoers demanding their money back. I moved my gaze from the limp piece of pink flesh and remarked, "That's it? That's why Mom makes the boys wear towels to the shower? That's it?" I suppressed a giggle. It looked something like a cold hot dog that wasn't good enough to be part of an Oscar Meyer eight-pack. Which reminded me: I hadn't eaten lunch yet. Suddenly, I was extremely hungry for PB&J.

I made a mad dash for the exit and ran for my life from the Gold's backyard – or as fast as one can crawl under dying fruit trees and prickly bushes. Billy yelled through the jungle, "Hey, let me see yours! Get back here! Let me see what you've got hidden inside those shorts, Maclyn Mills!"

Nearly out of the gate, I remember yelling back, "Well, it sure isn't as silly as what you've got hanging between your legs, Billy Gold!"

I reached Paisley's front door breathless and rang the bell.

"Eliza, where have you been? You know I don't like waiting around. Why are you panting? Oh, come in and tell me. I made us some yummy sandwiches with my mom's delicious peach jam. And we have iced tea with fresh lemons that Billy's mom brought by this morning. I hope you're hungry."

"Am I ever."

So that was my first glance at the male unknown. Having that curiosity satisfied – for the time being – I thought I might be able to fully concentrate on more important issues.

However, my encounter with Billy and his curiosity tent only served to encourage further thoughts about boys and such. I wanted to know more. Dad always said you learn through experience.

Ewww, I thought. I'm not ready for that.

12

A HIS-TOE WHAT?

So Mom's still clear across the country and I'm pretty much left helping out around the house – laundry, dishes, cooking, vacuuming. The boys help some, but January includes the collision of basketball and football. This typically leads to an empty home, overflowing laundry baskets, and hungry dinner diners.

As my heart swells for Grandpa and Mom, I feel a different tug for Joe Basketball. Unfortunately for me, there's no one here for girl talks.

I've always wanted a sister. I love my brothers, but there come times in a girl's life when she needs another girl's opinions and advice. There's Paisley, but she's more of a pal and knows little more about life than I do. As far as everyday growing up problems go, Pais hasn't the time. Especially for silly things and girlish thoughts, like boys, periods and padded bras.

She says she's too busy with more important matters, mostly the organization. But of late, she's been spending much of her valuable time at the library reading books by authors whose names I can't even pronounce, let alone understand what they're saying.

I'd be too embarrassed to talk to Eric about 'girl' things,

and whenever I even mention boys or bras to Mom, she changes the subject quickly, so quickly I often don't realize that we are soon discussing what kind of cheese to put in tonight's lasagna. So skilled has she become at this that I easily forget my original reason for coming into the room.

If only I had a sister, preferably an older one. One who could tell me what happens to a girl as she grows up. What happens to her body? Her mind? What she should expect? Should ignore?

Yes, an older sister would be very useful.

Since Mom's had her operation, there won't be anymore baby Mills arriving. Mom had a hysterectomy about a year ago. I was heading into my 11th birthday and hadn't any courses in sex ed, so Dad, who knows as much about the workings of the female body as Plato knew about twin-engine jets, tried to explain Mom's situation to me.

Fall 1976, age nearly 11, home

Dad walked into my bedroom the afternoon of mom's operation carrying a tape recorder in his chapped hands. I hadn't noticed him until he was sitting down next to me. I was reading "The Cat That Ate My Gymsuit" for the hundredth time.

A pair of brown cotton-covered legs appeared at the corner of my eye. Dad sat upright next to me with his large fireman's hands placed silently atop the black plastic tape recorder.

"Hello, Mac, whatcha doin' there?" When Dad was nervous, he'd speak as if he were just about to cough. So during the whole conversation, you constantly want to clear your own throat, feeling that catch that never quite breaks away.

"Oh, I'm just ... nothing really, just reading, you know." I looked curiously at the tape recorder then up at Dad who stared blankly at my book and the brown Coca-Cola stain on the cover just below the title. I fiddled with the soft cover's edges, bending the weaker parts this way and that. Suddenly, I could feel the weight of the book. I rubbed my hands over the edges of the closed pages, feeling the smoothness created by their togetherness, and that little bit of tickle from the uneven trim of each individual page.

"Uh, what's with the tape recorder?"

"Tape recorder?" he repeated, sounding as confused as me. Then he looked at me and blinked his tired eyes. Firemen work these crazy 24-hour shifts. Dad would leave just as we woke to get ready for school and return the next morning as we were heading out the door the following day. He'd sleep while we were in school and be up when we got home.

On those days, we'd get a groggy, sometimes cranky, dad. By the next day, he'd be back to his regular self then off on the schedule the following morning. Somehow, we all got used to it. However, in September and October, the real intense fire seasons, after a long dry summer, we might not see Dad for days.

Living in the desert valley, near the mountains and some really hot areas, firemen were sure to work lots of overtime just before fall. That's probably another reason I like fall, with the cooler weather, and some rain coming in, Dad's home more often and not so tired from busy shifts fighting fires.

He ran his fingers along the edges of the black plastic recorder, itself nearly the size of one of his large warm hands. "Well, see, I, uh, wanted to talk about something important to you. Something serious. Well, not serious, you know, in the sense of, uh, serious." Good start, Dad. "It's about your mom. You know, why she's in the hospital and all." He swallowed. "Has anyone told you why she's there?"

"No." I shook my head. "No one's really said anything. Just Kenny said she'd be home soon and I shouldn't worry, it was a routine thing."

"Well, he's right. You don't need to worry, it is sort of a

routine operation, not like an emergency, like an appendix or something." He fumbled with the tape recorder. He was nervous. To say the least.

Two years ago I couldn't understand why, but now I can appreciate his hesitation in talking with me. It was kinda like telling your daughter about sex; but here was a father trying to explain to his not-yet-11-year-old little girl why her mother would never bring her a sister.

"Mom's in the hospital to have an operation," Dad continued with renewed confidence. "She's having a hysterectomy."

"A his-toe what?"

"A hysterectomy. It's when women get older, and they, um, their body, um, gets tired of having babies. You know." He paused to smile. "Do you understand, Mac? Mom won't have any more kids now. You're the last. I mean we weren't planning on having any more kids, anyway. We've got five of you. So, that's it. No more brothers, no sisters."

"I guess five kids is kind of a lot, anyway. Still, I would've loved a little sister or something, but five kids, yeah, that's a lot." I smiled. Lifting one of his large, soft hands, I held it, kind of shaking it. Then I put it to my face. "Thanks for telling me Dad."

"Yeah. Um, I guess I could tell you a little more about the operation. So, um, let's see, you remember Daisy, your beagle? One day Kenny and I took her to the vet, and when we brought her home she had a big white bandage wrapped around her stomach. Remember?" I nodded. "Well, Daisy had a hysterectomy. We told you she was fixed, which meant I, uh, we, wouldn't have to worry about lots of little Daisys running around the kitchen floor. So that's kind of what the doctor is going to do to Mom. She's going to be fixed so that she won't have any more pup-, kids, I mean. So she won't have any more kids."

Dad suddenly stood up as if he'd just remembered something terribly important. He didn't say anything for several minutes, just walked thoughtfully to the window, staring blankly outside at the sky, one of those Denny's skies, the colors of pink and orange swirling around wisps of clouds. Dad stood silently in his soft yellow cardigan, which hung loosely off his shoulders because of so many washings and children's tuggings. Then he turned back 'round to me.

"See this tape recorder, Mac, this tape recorder works perfectly. It plays, rewinds, stops, and all that stuff. But because it's also a radio, you don't need a cassette for it to be useful. See?" Not really, but I let him continue. "If you have a cassette, then you can tape conversations and things. And later, you can play them back and reproduce those moments. But if you don't have a cassette, if someone takes it away, you can't reproduce things any more, even though all the buttons still work. So the recorder still works, and the radio still works, and ... do you see what I'm saying?"

"Well, I think so," I was afraid to tell him he sounded more like a Kodak commercial than my dad. He'd like everything to fit into neat little packages that never tore or unraveled, and he couldn't tell a story unless he had some little analogy, some symbol to compare, to help him out.

Dad didn't trust his own words. That firefighter in him needed a team to battle every blaze, no matter how big or small.

"But, um, what does this all have to with Mom?"

"Well, that's what I'm getting to." He sat back down on the bed and turned to me. "See, Mom isn't, well, she's, she's your mom, right? And, she's had you, she's had you and your four brothers. And, but, to do this, to have children, a woman needs certain parts, you know, and um that's what helps make the baby. Actually, these parts help the baby ... no, they, um, they give the baby a room to grow in before it's ready to come out. Well, if these parts aren't working properly, then the doctor takes them out. Like the cassette," he popped open the recorder and pulled out the cassette.

I suddenly had this horrifying image of the doctor popping open Daisy's stomach and pulling out some piece of machinery. And Mom, this is what they were going to do to her?

"So, Mac, what it all boils down to, really, is Mom's having her cassette removed. Of course, she still will be able to do all the things she does normally, you know, just not have anymore kids."

"Like the tape recorder still works without the cassette. It's just that you can't record anything, but you can play other tapes?" I struggled to make sense of this strange analogy.

"Exactly! Good." Dad stood up, heaved a heavy sigh, and, satisfied with his roundabout explanation, walked to the door. Then he turned, looked back for a moment, and asked if I wanted to go down to the hospital with him and the boys. I said I did.

He walked over to me, kissed me fatherly on the head, stroked my hair, smiled as if he were going to say one more thing, then turned and walked out.

Not ever being able to have a sister saddened me. But I did have my mom and one very determined dad (with some really strange explanations).

Hospitals. It's where I entered the world and where Grandpa left it. For most, I guess, hospitals are the weigh station of life and death.

13

PINECONE POND

Death isn't a moment I want to hold close to, but it somehow clings like Velcro to your soul.

I remember the last time I was with Grandpa. When he died, at that next moment, I just shut my eyes, removed my hands from beneath his withered one and took it inside mine, stroking the thin fingers and thinking about his wise old words. *Wise. Old.* Traveling companions through time. I wondered if one couldn't be young and wise, or if she had to wait until the years passed before one day she was old. Then in a few days, she would be WISE. And people would call her the old wise woman.

The Old Wise Woman of Santa Nina. That's who I would be one day.

However, I thought, I didn't want to have tubes in me dripping gooey yellow liquids into my body, or pulsating TV sets at my bedside. Could one, I wondered, be old and wise without pain, without hospitals, without stiff white dressing gowns and silvery bedpans? Could one just be old, or just wise?

Gently, I placed Grandpa's hand by his own side on the yellowed blanket. I turned 'round and there, in the doorway like two lifeless statues, stood Mom and Grandma. A warmth rushed through my body, and I wondered how long they'd been standing there or what they'd heard. The two mothers walked toward us. Grandma kissed my forehead then pulled up a chair to the other side of the bed, sat down, and took Grandpa's hand and stroked it like I had. Mother leaned over and kissed his wrinkled forehead then whispered to me that we were leaving.

I walked around the bed, kissed and hugged Grandma then said to her, "Don't be lonely, Grandma, even when he's gone, I know he will always be close to you. Remember to listen for him. That's what he would want you to do."

She smiled and nodded her fragile head as if she'd already known this, as if she really did know Grandpa would never completely leave her. And then I knew too, that she would never be lonely. I bent over, kissed Grandpa's soft cheek, and whispered in his ear, "I'll be listening for you, too, Grandpa."

It's funny – loss. It's not just death that conjures up this sadness. Other events take me there, too. Sometimes, with friends, when you fight that emptiness emerges. It's a horrible feeling that washes over me. I've experienced it with Paisley, and I didn't like it one bit.

Summer 1977, age 11 and a half, Pinecone Pond

A typical hot August day in Santa Nina, and Pais and I decided to ride our bikes up to Pinecone Pond, some three miles away just before the inclined highway up the Santa Nina Mountains. We pedaled under a burning sun, anticipating the cool refreshing treat that awaited us.

Pinecone Pond did not disappoint. The desert sun shone down upon the cool, murky green waters. So bright the sun was that you might have thought it'd burn all that dazzling water away.

Pais and I began by dipping our toes. Trouble was, in all

our excitement to get up to the pond early, neither of us had brought our swimsuits. And we weren't about to skinny dip. Unable to resist the temping waters, we jumped in fully clothed. The refreshing liquid soothed our hot skin but waterlogged our shorts, T-shirts and tennies. Soggy clothes made no difference to us.

We splashed about for a while, until Pais discovered she could float on her back. I tried it and we lay there as the pond's cooling waters rippled over our grateful bodies. Closing my eyes to the blinding sun, I savored this peaceful moment. Then, as usual, Paisley broke the silence.

"Eliza, do you ever wonder where we come from? I mean, originally. I've heard the whole creation story about Adam and Eve and the whole evolution thing with monkeys and stuff, but I don't get-"

"Yeah," I interrupted, "Roger Thomas definitely fits the evolution thing, definite monkey material there-"

"Eliza! Stop! I'm being serious. Come on, for just a moment, don't make jokes."

"Okay, no jokes, but come on, don't you think Roger's got some monkey blood going on there?" Roger Thomas, a tall skinny pale-faced kid suffered the misfortune of being born with ears that stuck straight out of his tiny head. Because of his height (I mean he had to have been nearly 5 and a half feet at 10 years), his arms dangled at his sides while he walked the halls. No one ever called Roger "monkey" to his face. You just don't go calling names to kids who are almost a foot taller than you. Besides, Roger was a pretty cool guy.

"Eliza, really, you never take anything seriously. Picking on Roger Thomas, of all people."

"But, Pais, c'mon, I was jus-"

"The guy couldn't be sweeter than jelly," Paisley continued, now standing and glaring at me, hands on hips, occasional finger wagging in shame. "Did you know that he volunteers at the animal shelter? His mom works there. He even..."

The rest of her lectured words trailed away. It was as if

someone had turned off the sound but left the picture playing. I watched her finger-wagging and hip-gripping hand stances as she walked from the lake toward the shore, seemingly more interested in ranting than caring about my reaction. The whole time she was yelling at me, looking up at the sky, and flailing those arms and fingers. I at first remained still in the shallow pond, stunned and stinging from her response, but then I decided to follow her back to shore hoping for a chance to redeem my failings.

As a warm wind blew down from the mountains, I followed Paisley's path out of the pond, considering how to construct some sort of apology. Yet as soon as we reached the shore and looked up at each other, we broke into hysterical laughter, doubling over with sidesplitting barks and snorts.

It wasn't the argument about Roger Thomas that sent us into fits. Pais and I had both worn white T-shirts and white shorts. And the water had worked its transparency with our outfits. You could see EVERYTHING! I mean we might as well have gone skinny-dipping.

Raisins in the sun. That's what peaked out beneath our soaking white T's. Embarrassment led to laughter and laughter just led to hysterics. After the giggling fit, we tried to ring out our shirts and pull them away from our bodies. Then we lay on the warm carpet of grass while the sun tried to dry us before we returned home. I certainly didn't want to run into John F half-nude.

"We need to figure this out, Eliza. I need to know, I need to find out the answer or answers." We mounted our bikes.

"What, you mean where we came from and all that? You're still trying to figure that out? Well, try all you want. You're not going to, Pais. We're not going to know anything until we die." And as soon as the words escaped my lips, I added, "Which I hope to be many, many, years from today!"

"When we die. Yeah, I see," she pedaled faster, obviously in deeper thought, meaning the whole Roger Thomas thing was history for now. "Do you think then, that when we die, we keep living in a different world?"

"Whaddya mean? Like ghosts? I'm not spending my death floating around the dusty closets of an old deserted house. Ghosts scare me. How could I be a – how could I be something I'm afraid of? Oh no, no way, no ghosts for me, too scary."

"No, no, Eliza! See, this is where you are so wrong. You said you thought that we would probably not know anything until we died. Right? Remember saying that?" I nodded against my will. "That must mean that you think we'll enter another world."

"You mean like the Twilight Zone or something? And we either go to Heaven, or um, you know, the place down there; and we're either angels or devils; and if we're angels, we help people? Like in that one episode where the angel tried to help Carol Burnett from being such a klutz, and then he-"

"Eliza, I am trying to be serious, and I am trying to be patient with you." Oh, here comes the mother tone again. Her words spun faster than her wheels. "This is important, and I'm sick and tired of you and your dumb sense of humor! This isn't television. This is Life! Life, Eliza, remember?"

Yep, she sounded just like Linda, but I wasn't going to be the one to point that out. So I remained silent.

"I don't know if we'll go to Heaven or Hell – you can say that word, Eliza. I don't even know if those places exist. I'm just saying that there must be something after this life, something good. Something where we don't have bodies."

"You mean we might just be a bunch of little heads floating around in space?"

"Eliza!" And she sped ahead of me; turning the corner of Long Street at a speed so fast, I was sure I'd find her sprawled on the pavement when I caught up.

I careened around that corner to find her still pedaling. Paisley rarely found amusement in my silly observations. This time, I'd clearly upset her. I wasn't sure at the time what I had actually done. And she wouldn't tell me.

Though silent the rest of the ride home, I knew Paisley still juggled those thoughts. *Where do we come from? Where will we go?* Way heavy thoughts for my 11-year-old head.

Paisley's anger worried me more. I wasn't being silly at the pond. Who knows what will happen to us when we die? Anyway, Roger Thomas did look like monkey.

As we rounded the corner home, I tried to think of something to say. We reached Paisley's house first. Hopping off her bike, Pais didn't even turn to say goodbye, she just rolled her bike up the cement driveway and pushed through the splintery wooden gate into her backyard. As it clicked shut, that familiar sensation of loss overwhelmed my body; like a sudden rush of cold wind stinging the hairs at the back of your neck.

Then like an empty jar on a windowsill, I felt it. Loss. I wished so much that Pais would appear at her front door. I stared at its black paint for what seemed like hours, believing I saw it open or heard a latch turn. Nothing.

I knew I hadn't lost Paisley as a friend, but I feared I'd done something even worse – I'd hurt her. Sliding off my bike, I continued the slow walk home. Goose bumps rose on my arms as the sun set. I wished the day could start all over.

I lay my bike on the sidewalk and ran over to my maple. I climbed up its scratchy trunk despite my bare legs. Up onto that arm, I sat there, watching the red sunset behind the brown mountains, feeling a bit gray and cold all over.

I didn't even notice Marc sweeping the front porch. Now Marc earned no medal of honor for keen observation, but anyone could see I was upset. He set down the broom, skillfully climbed up the tree, and sat next to me dangling his legs in rhythm to mine. He reached into his left pocket. A half-eaten Mars bar emerged. Handing it to me, he said, "Whatever it is, it's not worth it. Besides, tomorrow, you won't remember half of it. Life's just like that. Time takes care of what we can't."

Was that my shallow brother? The one who jokes at weddings and dinner?

I savored this rare moment of brotherly affection with Marc, and in a sweet way, it helped me feel not so bad about Paisley. The next day, he was right. I could only remember half of it, and Paisley acted as if nothing had happened at all.

How'd he know that?

14

OKAY, LET'S TALK ABOUT *THE* MOMENT

Not all awkward moments fade into the distance.

I remember watching Grandpa lying there in the hospital, tubes in his arms and legs, waiting to die. This memory sits coldly inside me like it happened yesterday.

I wonder if Grandpa wished he were young again. What's tougher, growing up or dying? I know each carries a burden, but I'm hoping that growing up leads to fun in the end.

How does a person enjoy being young and figure out Life's puzzles and great mysteries - especially when your body is announcing itself to the adult world? Especially when that body is female. Who wants to talk about hair and curves and, and, you know, periods? It's not quite dinner table conversation.

My brothers all safely escaped the change without so much as a razor nick. I distinctly remember two summers ago when 14-year-old Marc proudly ran shirtless around the neighborhood so that all the girls (and boys) could see his manly, hairy armpits.

Boys seem so much prouder when all these changes happen. Girls usually want to brag about being women then hide all the evidence.

Last summer, when a few scraggly hairs appeared inside *my* armpits, Mom gave me a razor and reminded me that I was now a lady. Why is it boys turn into men not gentlemen, while girls turn into ladies not just women? Paisley's 'liberated' mother nearly echoed mine with the Lady Schick, leaving Pais just as baffled.

Why such a fuss over our bodies? Young girls eagerly anticipate *the* moment, carrying pink-covered pads in their purses or pencil cases, "just in case," thinking a tiny stream of blood will start trickling down their leg in the middle of a history lesson.

Boys go into the bathroom every morning with magnifying lenses impatiently seeking out that first prickly whisker. They proudly show up at school with silly little wisps of nothing under their noses.

"See that," they boast to buddies in the hall.

See what? I always wonder. I want to shout, *Get a washcloth and clean that dirt!*

Yet when the periods and hair and everything finally do arrive, girls complain about cramps and search stores for miracle creams to clean up hair-in-places-it-shouldn't-be. Impatient to grow up.

Thinking about Grandpa, I doubt he ever wished he were young again. He seemed content to share what he'd learned along the way.

So where's this division between adult and childhood anyway? At what moment do I become a woman? Was it that December morning when I started my period? This past October when I turned 13? Or will it be in two years when I can drive? Is there a test to pass, a certain word to spell, or is it just the ability to stay up past midnight without yawning? Maybe a mythical sign appears, like a lightning bolt that strikes as you finish reading your first Shakespearean play.

That real moment must be waiting out in the cold; my only contact with it, a now-and-again glimpse through fogged up windows.

Christmas 1977, age 12, home

Two Christmases ago, a just-turned 12, Pais gave me her news.

"It started," she shared while folding up some wrapping paper she intended to reuse next year.

"What started?"

"It, you know. I got it." Clearly she found my inability to read her mind annoying.

"Uh, Pais, I don't know what you're talking about. You got what? A new book? The answer to something? What?" My hands flew around me like fireflies. *Tell me, tell me!* I wanted to shout.

"I got my period. That's all. No biggie." She flicked a smile my way and turned the subject back to outlining another animal rights poster for the gym. Subject opened. Subject closed. All in about the time it takes to fill a glass with water.

I stared at her, open-mouthed, shook my head then offered, "Congrats, I guess. Wow. So you got it."

"Yeah. Whatever," she returned. Yeah, whatever. Subject closed.

I told her I needed to get home for dinner, opened her door and ran out of that house. I didn't pause a moment to raise *the* subject at the dinner table. We ate, talked about nothing - sports mostly - cleaned up and the boys splintered off in their own directions.

I decided to make my way upstairs to Mom and Dad's room where they prepared to leave for a party at the Woods. I had to talk to Mom, though I held out little hope she could shed any light on my concerns.

As I approached their bedroom, I heard Dad singing "O Come all Ye Faithful" in the shower. Mom sat silently on the corner of her neatly made bed in her blue feathery bathrobe. The blinking lights of the television captured her gaze as Bob Barker invited, "Peter Williams, come on down!" Screams from the audience. The show could easily be mistaken for one of those Twentieth Century evangelical TV programs.

Mom sat hypnotized to the sermon-like product descriptions. Her neatly coiffed brown hair rested delicately upon her like a crown as she sat, hands folded, undisturbed. The temporarily unpainted face exposed eyes she never saw through unless decorated and lips she never kissed with unless colored. For Mother Mills - wife of a fireman captain, natural mother of five healthy children and 1975-1976 PTA president – rarely revealed her unpainted self to strangers, occasionally to children, only on Sundays to her husband, but never to herself.

"Mom, do you think I'm taller than I was last year?" Startled, she looked up then furrowed, her eyebrows forming the expected, confused what-on-earth-is-it-now-Mac expression. I moved toward a mark I'd made in their doorway last Christmas when I had just turned 11. "Could you check?" I held out a pencil to her.

"I can see that even in the past month you've grown, and of course your growing doesn't stop there." She looked back at the TV hoping for some help from Bob? This open-ended comment puzzled me, but I left it deciding to launch into my current dilemma, which I hoped had crossed Mom's mind recently.

How to bring up this delicate subject .... Paisley had started her period two days ago, telling me of this (what I'd thought to be) happy moment in a rather matter-of-fact way. That was Paisley, a very matter-of-fact girl. To me, however, the start of *that* period seemed overwhelming.

I felt helpless inside and didn't know if I would be able to handle such a queer happening in my tiny body. Surely Mom would share with me her feelings when she had begun.

"Have you noticed anything – different – about Paisley lately, Mom?"

"No," her gaze unbroken from the television. "She's a sweet girl, Maclyn. Have you met any new girls in class? Whatever happened to that tall girl ... Martha? Wasn't that her name? Such a polite young girl," her eyes never leaving the TV, her thoughts on autopilot not even paying attention to herself let alone me.

"How much did you say I'd grown?" I asked, trying to work my way up to my real question, hoping she'd suddenly turn to me and say, *Mac, you are such a beautiful young lady, I wouldn't worry about your body because nature takes care of everything. It will all be fine.*

Instead, eyes not moving, "I'd say about two inches since last Christmas. You will probably grow to be taller than me but not as tall as your brothers."

The sudden thought that I might actually never sprout beyond five-foot-five temporarily jerked me away from my real concern. For a moment, my mind wandered into the short world of the non-super model looking college co-ed who dated the short, bald engineering majors. I guess being taller than all of the sixth grade boys would soon change. Maybe John F preferred short girls. There had to be a silver lining here somewhere.

"Okay, Maclyn, I need to get ready for this party, and your father will be out of the shower soon. So, why don't you – "

My thoughts returned to my real worries, "Mom, I have to ask you a very, very important question!" My shouting surprised me more than her.

"Okay - what is it? But quickly."

"Well, it's about, um..." I mumbled as I moved forward into the room then set myself down softly on the bed next to her. I could still hear the TV babbling in the background ('next item up for bid...'). "I wanted to talk to you about ... about periods. You know, like when am I going to start? And, well, will it hurt? Tell me how long it lasts and all that, and what I ... I ... and, Paisley got hers already, and-"

"Slow down, honey. You're a big girl. Didn't you have one of those" (nervous pause) "courses in school last year or something?" I could tell Mom wasn't too keen on the subject with me. I felt so helpless and just wanted some motherly advice or a hug that said it would all be okay. Why was she making this so hard for me?

"Just tell me, Mom, does it hurt?"

"No, it doesn't hurt. It's not like having a baby, if that's what you mean. Nothing is like having a baby. Now, come on, I don't want to be late for this party, and your father is out of the shower. He'll be wanting to come in here and get dressed." I put on my dejected look, the nobody-cares-about-me face of doom and gloom, the one that always works on Dad. "Maclyn, help me out a little here, will you? Get my grey stockings off the dresser there."

Sure, sure, what are daughters for? But Mom wasn't that out of it. She sensed my desperation.

"Funny, Grandma never wears anything but sheer silk stockings. She wouldn't be caught dead in grey ones. You don't really get much of a chance to talk with my mother, do you, Maclyn? Not that she'd probably have anything to say to you. She's difficult to talk with, if you know what I mean." Yes, Mother, I know exactly what you mean. "See, when I was your age, I had the same questions about, about my body, but Grandma was constantly changing the subject." Mom had on her stockings now, oblivious to any similarities between herself and her mother. "She never really let me ask the questions that I had in mind. I was so frightened of her, my own mother."

Imagine.

"Well, anyway, one day I discovered I had begun, you know..." With her back to me, she hooked her bra then shimmied into her beige slip. "Delighted I was, so, uh, I don't know, I felt like such a lady, and I ran into the kitchen to tell my mother. And, do you know what she did, Maclyn?"

"Hugged and kissed you and told you how much she loved you?" I ventured hopefully.

"She slapped my face."

"Slapped you?"

"It's a tradition in our family to slap the daughter for good luck. Sort of like, like the slap of life on the rump that you get from the doctor when you're born." She opened her closet and sifted through her department store collection of clothing. My mother stocked up on garments like people do on tins of food before a war. She chose a basic black polyester dress with a white-laced collar then turned to me, satisfied with her story, and said, "Now go on, honey, I really need to get ready."

I walked out completely dissatisfied, and a little horrified. Down the hall, in my bedroom, I sat in silence trying to make some sense of this "family tradition". Suddenly I realized she had never really answered my question. She had merely diverted me.

Well, it didn't work. I now sat with an image in my mind that wouldn't leave: being slapped. No one had ever slapped me before, but somehow I imagined that it would really hurt. Well, if I'm going to get slapped, then I just won't get my period at all. And if that meant not becoming a woman, well then that would just have to be. I didn't want a slap across my face. Growing up didn't need to be that painful.

Of course, that cold wintry day arrived in what seemed like only moments after I'd decided not to become a woman. But a girl has the right to change her mind, so I decided to grin and bear it. I would do it.

I did hesitate slightly in the kitchen that morning. I knew Mom was going to slap me, but I had started and she was my mother. Something told me she'd actually be happy for me. After all, I was her only daughter.

14 1/2

THE DAY

Okay, so let's get to the real moment here. You know, girls, it's *the* moment you wait on all through junior high.

There was nothing unusual when I started my period. Still, it's definitely a day I'll never forget, a day each girl curiously anticipates ever since the sex-ed lecture in that sixth grade PE class or in science or with your homeroom teacher. Wherever you first hear "the Talk" or see "the Film", it's a stamp on your brain like no other. And from that day, you wait.

Every time you go to the bathroom, you look. Every time you change your clothes, you look. And each time you are invited to a swim party, you worry: is this the day?

Unlike I had assumed, though, I didn't wake up that morning needing a B-cup bra or seeing the world in a whole new wondrous light.

On the outside, I was unchanged. No one would know that in a few hours, I would be bleeding.

On the outside, I was just plain old Eliza Mills. But within, I felt something growing, maturing, maybe out of my own elaborate imagination, maybe not.

Really, though, there was nothing extraordinary at all

about that cold December day.

The *Day, December 30, 1977, age 12, home*

It had rained hard every night that week, so when I awoke that historical morning and peeked out my bedroom window, I was not surprised to see a beautiful glistening stream traveling down the street's gutters, like hundreds of nomadic molecules venturing onward through the world.

How was I to know a similar stream had begun inside my own body? A stream of bright red blood like a river to freedom had begun its journey.

I stretched, yawned and climbed back into bed, anticipating a day filled with doing nothing. As I scooted my body into a position of slumber-like comfort, I felt something wet underneath me. I sat up and turned around, staring down at my white bed sheet in horror (yes, true shock, horror, fright).

There, perhaps the size of a quarter, not so perfectly formed, more of a Freudian inkblot, there it was. Unannounced. Unexpected. A dingy brown spot on my clean white bed. Calm down, I tried to tell myself. Why couldn't I shake the thought that I had done something wrong?

I stood up and slowly walked to my full-length closet mirror, turning my back I peeked over my right shoulder. Indeed, a matching quarter-sized bloodstain lay at the center of my white flannel nightgown. Female intuition told me not to worry. I relaxed. A bashful smile spread widely across my face as I turned fully before the *mirror mirror* at my wall.

You're a woman, now, Eliza, I thought to myself. I knew you had it in you. I put on my pink quilted robe to hide my newly found womanhood and ran across the hall to my mom's room. No one there. Next room. Marc and Kevin lay lifeless beneath matching blue quilts. Just as well, my exciting news would only have embarrassed them. Nobody up in the attic. Eric must have slipped out earlier.

I considered calling Dad at the station. No, best to just wait until someone wakes up. My hopes disbanded, I walked downstairs to the kitchen in the returned mood of any other school holiday morning. An unexpected vision greeted me. Mom. Reading the newspaper at the kitchen table like it was any other morning. This sight of my mother draped in her light blue feather-necked robe, eating a bowl of cornflakes offered some comfort.

"Morning, Mom," I announced as cheerfully as possible then kissed her cheek. "Anything in the newspapers today? Any big news?"

"No. Nothing special." Over her shoulder, I could see she was catching up on the latest gossip about David Soul. My parents loved *Starsky and Hutch*. Dad liked the firefighting scenes and telling us what was real and what was ridiculous. I just liked watching David Soul (and, so did my mom, I think). After several minutes, Mom looked up, noticing me. I smiled.

"What are you grinning at? Have I got some cereal on my lips or something?" Unaware of my secret-hiding grin, which held back my actual fear of the slap, I quickly sucked it in and walked over to the cupboard for some Frosted Flakes. "Macyln, do you want to go downtown with me? They're having a sale and I need to pick up something for Marc's birthday. You and Paisley don't have anything special planned, do you?"

"Uh, no," I suddenly remembered why I was down in the kitchen. I couldn't sit down and eat breakfast. I had to give her the news. "I need to tell you something now, though, see ... I ... uh, well, I started."

"Started what?" she asked without even looking away from the newspaper, as if I'd just begun some new assignment for school. Okay, so now I understood Paisley's bumbles.

"I got my period." The bland English class word hung in the air like a pair of wet diapers on a clothesline. I wasn't sure what to do next. I could feel my face heating up, ready to explode with embarrassment, fear. Surely I was blushing. Why not, red was the color of the day.

What I didn't realize while trying to ignore my embarrassment was the smile draped across my mother's face. A big, beaming smile, sans lipstick; brighter than ever. Pride. Before I knew it, my mother was standing in front of me, hugging me. Gripping my arms, really, like a proud father whose son had just hooked his first trout. "That's wonderful, Maclyn. That's just wonderful."

"Yeah? Okay then, go ahead," I closed my eyes. "It's okay, I'm ready. It's good luck, right?" I grimaced. "I can take it."

I stood for a few seconds; eyes closed, shoulders cringing, my face already tingling. But nothing happened. I peered open one eye then both.

"Oh, honey, I'm not going to slap you. I'm so happy for you. My little girl," she said still holding my arms. I couldn't remember the last time my mother had hugged me, really hugged me. "My little girl," she said again.

I moved in and pulled her toward me, laying my head on her shoulder. I never wanted to let go. Never wanted to let go of being her little girl, yet feeling that tug of wanting to grow up, be a woman, have a boyfriend, drive a car, share secrets; but stay protected, stay small and loved with no worries of getting old and wrinkled or being alone.

A push, a pull, a tug. I never wanted to let go of this woman, my mother, so warm, so full of living, such security, just in the holding.

She patted my back gently then moved away and held my arms, staring at me with a big closed-mouth smile. "I suppose we'll need to get you a few things then." She let go, picked up her cereal bowl and walked over to the sink. She headed upstairs for my supplies.

I stood there, alone, with my own bowl of soggy flakes, not moving until her return. "Hey, Mom," I yelled, knowing she was probably halfway down the hall by now, "Does this mean I can stay up till midnight!?"

*   *   *

As I discovered after those three cramped and uncomfortable days in December, it takes more than a box of sanitary napkins and a bottle of aspirin to transform a 12-year-old girl into a mature woman.

So my quest continues. When's that magical moment when I blossom into this WOMAN? Life was so easy as a kid with my afternoon tree-lying and weekend movies with my brothers. I was sure it could only get better, but now in my teen years, life seems more complex.

Life changes every moment, like a fallen leaf traveling down a mountain stream, pitched over stones, diverted onto rivulets, direction unknown. I pass through life as this passenger, waiting to disembark, wondering where I'll end up. As I journey downstream, I gather and collect.

For me it's information, pieces and pieces of information that I continuously try to fit together like a jigsaw puzzle with no finished picture to guide me.

15

OH BROTHER!

A year of periods later and I was sitting at my dying grandfather's bedside. Life tosses out moments often with such randomness; or are we just unaware of their connections?

November 28, 1978 – that was the last time I saw Grandpa. *Wow*. The last time. The last time I kissed his soft cheeks. The last time I held his withered hand. But it wasn't the last time I'd heard his wise old voice.

I still hear him whisper in my ear, telling me to believe in myself. Believe. Whatever direction my life takes will be the right one. So I wait – not patiently, maybe, but I wait – until that little voice within tells me what to do, gives me the go ahead.

Maybe that day when I know what it is I should do or be, maybe that day I will also be that wise woman. A truly wise woman. Or maybe I really will have to wait until I'm old, lived life long enough to gather the wisdom until my hair turns gray and my hands begin to shake. I wonder when it happened to Grandpa, when he realized he was old, and, if he felt wise to the world.

Or just plain old.

I just feel young, and little, and small. I always do. I wonder if I always will because I'm the little sister. Wow. I just realized something. Everyone is older than me – my parents, my brothers, my aunts and uncles. There's no one younger. I'm it. That means that if life goes as it does, I'll be the last. I'll need to watch everyone grow old and die. Grandpa is only the beginning.

Growing up, not growing old. That's my plan. Perhaps a glimpse of my influences will shed light on why life confuses me so.

Marc, the youngest, 16, the comfort brother

Marc's closest in age to me, 16. He's over six feet tall but not quite as tall as Dad or Kenny. One phrase sums up Marc: girl-crazy. He has so many girlfriends, and they're constantly calling him on the phone, night and day! Sometimes, I think the phone was invented just for Marc because I don't think he'd exist at all without it.

Marc used to walk Paisley and me to school. I was so proud – that's my big brother, everyone, yep. He'd escort me and Pais to the gray wire fence, plant a small kiss on my cheek, take a few steps away, then turn back, flash half a smile and say, "Don't be rude to no one, Mac, and don't let no one be rude to you. And don't go anywhere after school. Wait for me. I'll meet you right here."

Across the yard to his buddies he'd run. Later, when he moved on to the junior high, he'd still walk us to the gate, give the speech then quickly jog across Park Way. Without fail, at ten to three, Marc'd meet Paisley and me to walk us home.

When I was seven and eight, I filled my entire day with thinking about meeting Marc after school and walking home with him. He'd usually have Eddie Hall with him, so we'd never have big talks like with Eric. I'd just have that big brother's here, it's all okay feeling, no matter what kind of day I'd had.

He'd hold each of our hands to cross the busy four-laned Vianova Avenue (and this is a guy who bought a backpack for his books just to free his hands to stick in his pockets).

Marc's my comfort brother. He's the guy people like to be around because he's just nice to be around. Everyone needs someone like that in life. Maybe that's why all these girls call my strange brother now.

None of my other brothers have as much of a fair-haired following of female groupies as Marc.

Kevin, the middle child, 18, the quiet brother

Next in line comes Kevin, 18, and in his first year of Junior College. Marc and Kevin used to be inseparable. Sharing a bedroom probably encouraged their friendship even more. You know, late night whispering, sneaking out the window (just Marc on that one). No pair of Mills' boys got along the way those two. I've never really understood why.

Kevin and Marc seem like two opposites. Kevin: timid as a mouse, girl-less, chronic studier, and very non-athletic. Marc: Mr. Jock, little league slugger since age eight, varsity swimmer at Santa Nina High School, and leader of the harem.

The only sport Kevin likes, if you can call it that, is Jazz. Not dancing, listening. He listens to his Jazz albums whenever the stereo's free, whenever, that is, Marc isn't blaring The Who or Rolling Stones.

One thing's funny about Kevin and Marc's relationship, though. Marc argues with someone in the house at least once a week, but I've never heard him even raise his voice at Kevin. I wonder if Kevin really doesn't ever do anything to bug Marc (except for correcting his grammar), or if Marc just has so much respect for Kevin and his notoriously straight-A school career that he lays off. I don't really think it's the grades, though, because Kenny has the same clean record.

Eric, 20, the thinker brother

If I were to name my favorite brother, it would without a doubt be Eric. Of course, I love all four of them equally (well, *equally* meaning for different reasons). Eric's just the only one who's ever taken time to talk with me. Really talk. And when we talk, I can tell he's not just trying to amuse me. It's not nice when someone talks to you just to pass the time. Eric would never do that to anyone, but that's the only way I think Kenny knows how to talk.

Kenny and Eric have probably exchanged even less words, and only one year separates them. Really, I don't think age has anything to do with it. It all has to do with wavelengths. Let's face it, Kenny doesn't have many. Marc's wavelengths don't seem to match Eric's very often either. Kevin is about the only brother who can talk with Eric.

Actually, Kevin gets along with just about everyone he talks to; whereas Eric only talks to people he gets along with. For me, talking to Eric is easy, almost like talking to Grandpa.

He never gets angry, only sits patiently and listens attentively, and he always shares the best advice. Sometimes I think he likes to tell people what to do; but really, he just has lots of opinions and ideas, and he likes to share them. And he likes to hear what other people think. That's unusual for my brothers. Take Kenny, who proudly hung a "Godfather" poster on his wall for years that read: When I want your opinion, I'll give it to you.

Kenny, the oldest, 21, the responsible brother

Kenny is a mini Dad. He's one of those busy kinds of people who you never know what they're being busy with. The kind who when he's sitting down watching the TV and you ask him a question at the commercial, he tells you he's busy. Or the kind who's eight years older than you and tells you, because of that, the two of you have nothing in common, nothing to talk about, even though that eight-year difference merely makes him an older brother and you a younger sister. And nothing more. I'm certainly glad Kenny wasn't twins.

Clearly, he resembles Dad. Physically speaking that is. Like Dad, Kenny's tall and thin, speaks with a deep rough voice and has that same sort of catch in his throat when he's nervous or not sure about something. They're so alike. I've even mistaken one for the other on the phone. The only real noticeable difference, as I mentioned earlier, would be the streaks of red in Kenny's flat hair. Dad has begun to show some streaks of gray. ("It's the smoke that colors my hair," he jokes.) Why should someone admit to getting older?

Dad's been a fireman for 20 years. I can't remember a night when I've gone to sleep without the woodsy smell of smoke tickling my nose. That's another difference between Dad and his eldest son. Kenny would never be a fireman, and Dad wouldn't be anything but a fireman. I think he's put a firebug in Marc, but Kenny'll never have it. For one, he doesn't like getting dirty. He says he prefers working with his mind, not his hands. (Whatever that's supposed to mean.) He's chosen what he calls a more "practical profession".

He finished his business degree last May at Santa Nina State. Since then, he's been working as a supervisor in the Sears men's section. He takes care of things like checking stock and making sure they're selling popular items. Sounds kind of boring to me, still Kenny boasts that it's an important job and that he's lucky to get it right out of college. He plans on moving up the chain of command.

How ordering men's underwear can ever be called "important", though, is beyond me. After a few years, he should move up to chief underwear orderer. Of course, he probably won't tell the family for a while, saying he'd been so busy he'd forgotten.

I think I can safely say right now, Kenny won't change much. He's always been a rather secretive person, spending most of his time locked away in his room, studying and reading, or so he'd tell us. We all learned not to disturb him in there because even a knock on the door to announce dinner received a promising threat of body part damage. Serious damage could be incurred during finals.

The only person who could enter Kenny's attic bedroom was Siamese Twin, Brad Gilton. Best friend, confidante and supreme goofball. Supreme-o-rama! This inseparable friendship began sophomore year at Santa Nina High, carried on through college, and (now this is creepy) continues today while they date the McQuinn Twins.

Two months ago, Brad and Kenny rented an apartment. Kenny had been working at some law offices downtown, just being a go-for for the big chiefs. Then he heard about the amazing underwear supervisor job. (Mock I may, this job pays him enough to live on his own.)

So a further benefit – not having to see Brad Gilton's goofy grin daily. Every time he'd come over, he'd pat my head like a little dog, saying, "How ya doin' there little one?"

Now Eric stays in the attic. At first, Kevin thought he'd get the coveted top floor because Eric made promises of moving out, too. Eric said to me, "Twenty-year-old boys shouldn't still be living at home." But he didn't have enough money to rent his own place (no sorting underwear for him), so he's stuck here at least until next summer.

Marc and Kevin had shared a room with Eric ever since they were toddlers. Marc had roomed with me until I turned four and was old enough to look at naked little boys and say, "What's that?"

I'd say this is one of my few advantages for being the only girl - I am assured my own room.

16

A CIRCLE OF SISTERS

Deep conversations usually involve Eric, but some topics are more suited for a sister. My emotions don't always flow easiest with Eric. I often imagine sister-time talks with Paisley. However, she's not always the best substitute either. Emotions don't flow smoothly with that girl.

If only I had a sister … . If I did have a sister, I might understand these crazy feelings inside me. Feelings about death and boys and everything. One minute I'm scared, the next I'm curious, the next I don't feel anything. What gives?

Believe. I hear you, Grandpa. I'm trying.

Group member rundown

I guess my sister-wishing explains my gathering a circle of girlfriends in my life. Our organization, the one Pais started, consists solely of girls. Now in eighth grade, we are a strong group of six. Since the group sort of evolved out of Paisley's desire for change, I just lucked out. Of course, Pais is sister-free, too.

Our first member joined six weeks after that late night meeting on Paisley's shag carpet in 1976: Amy Combs, an extremely smart yet shy girl in our sixth grade science class.

She's got a funny sense of humor. Actually, she hardly has any sense of humor; but there's something nice about her that makes you like her anyway. She doesn't laugh at jokes or tell them. She doesn't laugh at other people or even join in the fun others are having at someone's expense.

Amy really looks like a nice person. Describing her is just like describing a lollipop: round face, tall thin body, tees in different colors. Her Shirley Temple curly brown hair frames her circular face; a librarian's pursed smile, thick-but-not-coke-bottled round wire glasses, and three tiny freckles on an average-sized nose. Amy is probably the smartest person I know. Except for Eric, and maybe Paisley. Anyway, she's pretty smart for a teenager. As quiet as Amy Combs is, though, she's my favorite member of the group.

We next recruited artsy Heather Rose from our Halloween leaflets. Pais and I have always celebrated our birthdays jointly with a big Halloween Costume Party Bash, but when we turned 11 in sixth grade, we decided that was kid's stuff. We started dressing up in witch costumes and passing out candy at Paisley's house, inconspicuously dropping information leaflets about the organization into selective girls' bags.

Heather, being Miss Art Student, wore an elaborate witch costume, which she had constructed herself, all the way down to the pointy vinyl black shoes, crookedly pointy black velvet hat with dangling spiders, tattered black satiny cape and a staff made of an old umbrella cane. She accompanied her little sisters, eliciting giggles from them every time she cackled.

That witch costume mocks Heather's sweetness. You see, she's a candy striper, so she spends nearly every Saturday morning up at St. Dino's children's ward crafting stained-glass paper windows or felt hand puppets with kids tethered to IV's or wheelchairs. Heather signed up the day before Back to School night after viewing Paisley's art class self-portrait depicting her with an orange-feathered chicken in one arm and a plate of vegetables in the other. Above her pastel portrait was inked: "Pet a chicken, don't eat it."

Maybe we all dress up in witch costumes to conjure up some magic we hope will cure the world. Well, have you ever put on a witch's hat and felt that power, that enchantment, or that thrill that you could summon up something mystical and wonderful? I just love that.

Lisa Mitchell and Shelley Newman joined last year. (I'll tell you about them later.)

It's amazing actually that any girl gets in. Paisley checks out each recruit's character and background. I mean – *really* checks out. Sure, there's talking to other kids, asking our families if they know anyone in their families, and sneaking into the attendance office for a peak at their school records (that's my favorite part; it just takes a distraction of Ms. Bants with a plate of Paisley's mom's homemade peanut butter cookies). We've only had to turn one girl away, Carolyn Wells. Her dad was a butcher.

Pais always conducts the interviews, and I take notes. Both Amy and Heather sat in on Lisa and Shelley's interviews. Still, it's Paisley who gets to do all of the talking. Yeah, it's a little power trip for my friend who despises power. Contradictions, remember.

We only came close to trouble once, last year when Sara Jacob's dad phoned Mr. Park after Sara'd shown him the flyer. He asked where she'd gotten it. Bob told Mr. Jacobs that he didn't know a thing about the group (true) and that it was a matter he should take up with Paisley.

Mr. Jacobs wasn't about to talk to some kid about her silly club, so we never heard from him. In fact, Sara seemed to avoid us in the halls at school, too. Paisley swore an FBI-type looking guy was watching her house. I wonder if Charlie's Angels ever considered vegetarianism?

Anyway, the leaflets basically say things like: "Are you interested in protecting animals? Were you born in 1965 or later? Would you support laws to stop people from killing animals?" Then the girl wears a red T-shirt to school on a

Wednesday, and we find her at lunchtime.

Once, our silly friend Sarah decided to have some fun with Paisley Park. She wore a red T-shirt on a Wednesday – somehow having figured out the signal. However, on the back, she had written in black pen:

Bob's Burgers, home of the juiciest beef in town

Paisley did not find it funny at all. In fact, she didn't read the back until we interviewed Sarah.

See Sarah just wants to have a little fun, not take life so seriously. She's the kind of kid who when you just look at her, you laugh because you know she's going to say something ridiculous. Or, she'll smile and light up the room. You feel happy inside, and all you want to do is hear a joke or a funny story. There's simply something about her that makes me feel good to be near her. Sarah is the only girl to ever turn down being in our organization.

During her interview in Paisley's room, Sarah looked at Pais and said, "So you don't eat hamburgers because you think cows should be treated like us? But cows don't talk. They eat grass all day. It's not like they're saving up for retirement in Florida.

"I mean, what kind of plans can a cow really have? Yeah, uh, no, you see, I like hamburgers, and actually I like cows. I'll just say grace and eat my meat, girls, thanks anyway." Then she turned and strolled off.

I think she actually ticked off Paisley, but Pais just took out her little notebook and crossed off Sarah's name. "There (Sarah), who's next?" Still, I admire Sarah for being so sure of herself.

The organization has sort of bonded Pais and me for life. We're family in that way. Usually, Paisley's a pretty good substitute for a sister. Especially in the summer when my brothers and their music and their ball games and their yelling are all just a bit much. Pais helps me escape from these male get-togethers.

Except for the first two weeks in August. That's when the Parks take their family summer vacation - typically, a drive down to Las Palimas to visit Linda's sister's family.

When Paisley isn't around to hang out, I have to find my own place for solitude. In Paisley's absence these past two summers, I found a new quiet spot: my old little league field in Pinewood Park. Trouble is, it has restricted hours: Monday and Wednesday afternoons after one and Tuesdays and Thursdays after three-thirty. I need to be out of there before five. Teams practice in the mornings and play games at night. Mid-day hours mean an unforgivable scorching sun.

For some, it could be quite lonely sitting up high in the empty stands, looking out on the open field. But this girl finds contentment with the golden finches' tuneful songs as my only sounds and companions.

Sometimes I climb over the wire fence and sit right in the center of center field. I can do plenty of thinking there, and if my imagination is working well, I can pretend to be sitting amidst a grassy green meadow out in the country with nothing but colorful butterflies and blue jays to accompany my somber thoughts.

Unfortunately, on those rare days when my imagination fails to answer this desperate call, I find myself encircled by amber-colored dragonflies and yellow-striped buzzing bees with pointed stingers.

Centerfield is no place for meadowlarks.

17

PAISLEY WRITES A LETTER

I wonder how everything's going in New York. Maybe I should write Mom a letter. It always seems so much easier to speak in writing than it does in person. Somehow courage emerges with a little distance.

I love to get letters more than writing them, thought. Paisley wrote me a letter once. Just this past summer - the first letter I'd ever received from her with postage. (School notes don't count.) Her family takes vacation every year in Las Palimas

Nothing compares to opening the mailbox and seeing a letter with your handwritten name on it hiding in between all your parents' boring bills.

Last summer, Paisley's cousin Patrick joined his boy scout troop's summer camping expedition to the Santa Nina Mountains, so Pais didn't have anyone her age to talk to. Not that freckle-faced Patrick was any consolation - so says Pais.

That's why today, I hold the only letter penned by my friend on one hot yet breezy visit to the Southern California coast. (I'm saving it. You never know if Paisley'll be famous one day. She might even call upon me to write her memoirs.)

Summer 1978, almost 13, Santa Nina's little league field

I received her letter in the morning mail on the Eighth of August 1978. Although I had hoped to read it on the privacy of my maple, I decided it required further distance from home. The ballpark would work.

I'd have to wait patiently until one o'clock before I could trek out to my peaceful valley and enjoy my best friend's thoughtful prose under a sunny (and a little smoggy) Santa Nina sky. A lengthy piece of prose it was (fortunately) for this bored adolescent on summer break. Two and one-half notebook pages long!

Just as Marc introduced Bruce Springsteen as the afternoon's stereo concert, the clock struck one and I was out the door before you could say Born to Run! A ten-minute bike ride to the field. No boys in sight. Not even a bat forgotten or jacket left behind. The park slept quietly, absent of male voices; the burning sun having purified the air of boyish activities.

Hopping off my flowered banana seat, I rolled my shiny Schwinn with its chipped pink frame and wide handlebars over to the fence. I think that was about the last time I rode that bike. In October, I graduated to a ten-speed – Marc's old one. One benefit of being a little sister – I never suffer from worn hand-me-down clothes, just the occasional used bike - with a brand new girl's seat, of course.

After chaining my bike to the fence, I climbed over and comfortably settled myself in centerfield, just in front of the Al's Hardware sign.

August 5, 1978
Las Palimas, California

Dear Eliza,
Do you realize that in less than three months we'll be 13? (Just a decade of youth, a few years in-between, now

we approach the unlucky 13.)

It feels time for us to pick a path, a road to travel. Which road shall we choose? Which road calls to us? How will we know if what we decide is right? Who will tell us? Who will tell us what this world is all about?

I've been talking with Aunt Mary about this, hoping she might help me out. She was, needless to say, little help, but she did offer me a list of authors I might want to read in a few years. They write, she said, about existence. On being alive and what it all means. When I come home, we can check out some of these books at the library.

I want to look up books on God, too. There is no other way to explain beautiful colorful birds, dramatic sunsets, or such destructive-creative forces like volcanoes. The earth is alive, Eliza, alive with the Goddess!

Aunt Mary believes that when we die, that's it, that's the end. What about beyond? What about why we are here? Isn't there more, isn't there a reason each of us spends time on earth? I believe there is more, Eliza. There must be.

Sitting on my aunt's porch watching these exquisitely colorful Las Palimas sunsets, I've decided a few things in my life. I have concluded that my involvement with the organization is one of the best things I can do right now. I want to spread the idea of protecting animals. I have been thinking how much I don't like when my dad preaches to me about what not to do, so I have decided I don't want to preach to people either. I want to find a way so that people see on their own terms that this is the right thing to do.

You know, I think I trust myself more lately, Eliza. I trust my intuition. Mom and Aunt Mary say women have natural intuition. I was thinking that turning 13, getting our periods, and all of that is bringing us closer to being real women, which is bringing us closer to really hearing our intuition.

I know you are starting to notice boys. Well, I just want to say, please don't let them take you away from yourself, and what you want in this life. Keep your thoughts clear, in touch with Life and nature. I think, from being connected to the birds, the trees, the earth and all, we can grow into nicer people. Don't you agree?

Las Palimas is so beautiful, Eliza. We are right on the beach. Every morning I awake to the sound of the ocean. I love it! It's funny, we've been coming down here for years, but it wasn't until this summer that I really noticed the exquisite pink-red skies in the evenings. Maybe you could join us next year since John F doesn't come with us any more. Besides, you are just as much part of the family as Artemis. And she hasn't missed a summer yet. No one will have to let you out at night, either!

Your friend,
Paisley

I refolded the letter, returned it to its white envelope then placed the contents inside my blue jeans' back pocket. The blinding desert sun shone with such purpose from its lofty seat in the sky that I decided a lie-down in the warm grass was needed. My eyes closed in upon Paisley's deep words. As usual, her question-filled thoughts had piqued my own. I appreciated her curiosity and decided to contemplate it myself. It was all about being curious, not afraid. That's what I got from her letter.

Curiosity would warm the journey.

Nearly to the day that I had met Paisley, I knew an adventure had begun. What I am beginning to realize now, some 9 years later, is that our life's adventure actually begins the moment we're born, but it often takes something outside to awaken us to the wonders. Once awoken, though, we can grab the reigns and steer our life in any direction we choose.

Maybe that's why it took me so long to understand something - that the point wasn't merely to find answers but to continue asking questions, to keep asking others questions, and to keep asking ourselves. To keep wondering and never just accept things, to always be curious. I think that's one thing Grandpa was trying to explain.

Listen to those voices, he had said. Listen to the thoughts

underneath the surface, like unseen guides pointing me in the direction that will bring me home.

At 13, I still struggle to "get it", but I know I will. One day. When I was 10 and 11, most kids didn't talk about life the way Pais and I did. Most older people would say we were too young to "get" life. Maybe that was their way of not talking about something they didn't "get".

People don't want to be reminded about what they don't understand.

Other kids mock Paisley when she brings up stuff like the Goddess or All That Is. "Intellectual phony," they tease. Just jealous, I say. If only these teen-aged finger-pointers realized the irony in their accusations. Prancing around school in the latest trendy clothing and sneering at those who don't; boys in their "macho" cut-off shirts, and girls masked behind first-time make-up attempts. They mock Paisley? They don't know. I know.

Paisley Park is the most honest person I've ever met in my whole life. Nothing like those cruel gossipy girls.

I wish Pais really were my sister, but I suppose it doesn't much matter because she lives next door and we spend nearly every waking minute together. Best of all, we don't need to share a bedroom or hand-me-downs. Since I don't have an older sister, Pais is as good as the real thing.

Still, an older sister might have been useful. At the least, it would have provided another female voice to echo amongst this deep-pitched household. Of course, a few hand-me-downs thrown in that didn't resemble Dennis the Menace's wardrobe wouldn't hurt either.

Anyway, Mom must know most of the things a young girl needs to know. All that's needed by me is a little prodding for the information. If anything comes up in the future, I'll ask my mom.

18

SAMMY AND EMILY, A LOVE STORY

I talked to Mom this morning. She'll be home in three days. That's good. Getting tired of quesadillas and pasta. She put Grandma on the phone. We talked a bit.

"How are you, Grandma?"

"Just fine, dear, just fine."

Silence. "Are you settling in? How's Uncle Bert?"

"Yes, that's good. He's good. My boy. We are fixing my room."

"Ah, that's nice, Grandma. What color is it?" It seemed like an important question.

"Yellow." Good answer. I was hoping for something cheery.

"How's Mom, Grandma? Is she helping?"

"Oh, yes, your mother is helpful, and so is Ben."

"Uh – you mean, Bert?"

"Yes, him, too." Was she talking about Grandpa? I had to ask.

"Is Grandpa there, too?"

"Well, of course, he's always here." Oh, okay, I got it.

"That's good, Grandma. It's nice to hear your voice. Can I talk to Mom?" My mom took the receiver. I could hear

Grandma still talking in the background. To Grandpa? Maybe to Uncle Bert.

"Hey, Mom. Grandma sounds good."

"She is. Everything at home is good?"

"Yeah, we're fine. Almost to the end of your frozen dinners. We had the spinach lasagna last night. It was yummy."

"That's good, dear. Well, it's late here. I'll be home Friday, okay?" I could hear Mom's tiredness. I wanted to ask about Winnie, about having, not having a sister, but I decided against it. I was sure they'd discover some of her stuff.

"Okay. See you then. Bye."

Sometimes words don't reveal what's said. In that short conversation about practically nothing, I felt relieved. I felt Grandpa. He's still here.

It comforts me to think Grandma is home with her two kids. I like that. I like that Grandpa is still around her. They were so in love.

I remember talking to Aunt Sue last September and she was telling me about how she and Uncle Henry are still in love. It's weird to think about: *adults in love.* Actually, it's not what we started to talk about. I had called her into my room to talk about something more important.

S – e –, you know....

September 1978, almost 13, home

"I see, so you want to talk about that? With me? Well, I thought your father said that you had a sex ed course and all that last year or sometime – in sixth grade wasn't it? Isn't that right?" Aunt Sue's enthusiasm was less than I'd expected. And, obviously, my innocent invitation up to my bedroom after Dad's birthday dinner wasn't what she'd expected either.

"Yeah, two years ago in sixth grade. I had the class and

saw the films. You know, the ones with Sammy Sperm and Emily Egg. So, basically, I'm familiar with the parts. I just want to know when do I put it all to use, you know? When's the right time and who's the right person and all that stuff that they don't tell you in school."

"Well, aren't you straight-forward." Aunt Sue repositioned herself on my pink and white quilted bedspread. "So, you want to know how will you know that special boy to love? Is that what you're asking?"

"Yeah, that's it."

"Oh, Maclyn, honey, don't you trust yourself who'll be right? And, well, after all, dear, you are only 11."

"Twelve. I'll be 13 next month."

"Yes, 12, almost 13. But still, well, you're so... you have so much time ahead of you when you'll learn all of this," she paused and cast a curious smile toward me. "Is there someone special right now?"

"A boy?" I thought of John F, Eddie Hall, and, yuck, Billy Gold.

Then I remembered Joe Basketball.

"Yes, is there a special boy for you right now? In school, in the neighborhood, or somewhere?"

"Oh, I don't know." I twisted my hands together and bounced once on the bed. "I mean, all the boys I know are just, you know, just friends. Or pests. There's no one special. Not really. When did you know Uncle Henry was right for you?"

I just couldn't tell her about Joe. I haven't told anyone. I'm not even sure I like him. So he makes me melt when he passes. So I can't think straight when he's in the room. Does that mean I like him? That he's someone special?

Sitting next to me, Aunt Sue fidgeted with a gold chain around her neck and stared blankly at the thick pink shag carpet. Her navy blue polyester pants suit and white lace blouse draped her body; so typical of what she wore teaching high school English. Although she and Uncle Henry had no children of their own, I always thought they'd be the best parents.

Suddenly, a smile appeared across Aunt Sue's soft face, crinkling the corn silk on her cheeks. I guessed she was thinking about Uncle Henry. Maybe about the first time they'd met, the very first time she'd laid eyes on him.

"Well, Maclyn, with Uncle Henry, I just knew he was right. I can't quite pinpoint any specific moment that I fell in love with him. Oh, I'd say it was just, it was like a soothing feeling that came over me every time I saw or spoke to him. He wasn't trying to impress me or anything; he was just so honest and kind, so real.

Soothing, huh? That sounds kind of like melting, doesn't it?

"Everything he did, and often in what he didn't do, set me at ease. More with Henry, it's in the not-doings, the moments when someone else's husband might pass through a kitchen, past a sink full of dishes, those are the moments that we don't have. Those are the kinds of moments when he stops and helps, when he just does something because it needs doing, knows that's what partners do, they do the things that need to be done. Henry is that. He is the guy that does what needs to be done in the moments when others might not.

"I'm sure that's how it is with your mom and dad. Have you ever talked to them about this? I bet your mom would say something similar."

Would she? I couldn't imagine that. "Yeah, I suppose so," I lied. I looked down at my feet, my white sneakers, more gray than white, hiding their out-of-the-box first day shoe color. It seemed that was how Mom and Dad's relationship has gone. Sort of gray. Beneath the ordinary everyday of their lives, there still exists the love they've felt for each other when they first met. They've just forgotten for a while. Something unseen covers up all those nice feelings, all that love.

Hmm. Five kids. Yeah, there's a lot of love somewhere.

There must be some secret way of knowing the real thing. *True Love.* I thought Aunt Sue would know all the secrets. Maybe there weren't any. Maybe she was right. Maybe it was just a feeling. A melty feeling. Just how Uncle Henry made Aunt Sue feel. I looked up at her.

"Does Uncle Henry still make you feel warm and nice?"

"Yes," she glanced out the window then turned back to me and smiled. "He still makes me feel as amazing as I felt with him 24 years ago. He even melts me now and again."

I froze. "Did you say he melts you?"

"Yeah, melts. He can just say something sweet and I feel like a puddle, a defenseless puddle. It's a lovely feeling."

Yeah, I know.

"So, melting, would you say that's love?"

Aunt Sue stopped her vacant stare out my window. She turned toward me. "Does someone melt you, Maclyn?"

It still seemed so confusing, this love thing. I was sure, also, that I wasn't understanding what Aunt Sue had said about s-e-. Actually, she hadn't said anything specifically about it at all.

"Umm, no, well, maybe, sort of..."

"Don't be afraid to melt a little, Honey. That's a good thing. It means you're willing to let your feelings through, instead of having your head sort them out. Melting is normal."

How reassuring.

"I think I see a little bit what you're saying about love, and how you know the person's right for you. But, well, what about the rest?" She hadn't gotten to the important stuff. I wasn't letting her off the hook that easily. "Is that really the same thing? Like, when you know you're in love, that the guy's right, and it's time?"

Aunt Sue let out a loud burst of laughter and squeezed my knee. "Not quite, Honey," she said, then smiled. "I guess if you put it that way ... well, no, that's not exactly how it goes. Now, you know you are far too young to be thinking about something like, like sex." Apparently my brain hadn't gotten the memo, because almost-13-year-old girls think about this stuff. A lot.

I looked out my window at my maple. She seemed to be listening in on this fragile conversation. What might my majestic maple say about all this?

"Maclyn, did you hear me?" I looked over at my aunt. Where'd I go?

"Yeah, I was just thinking about you saying I shouldn't be thinking about this stuff. But, but –"

"I know. But you are. It's okay, Sweetie. Just remember, you're not quite yet 12, -"

"Thirteen," I corrected.

"Yes, not quite 13, and I don't want to tell you something different from what your folks might say. This is really something you should talk over with them."

"I've thought about that, but it's easier talking with you. Mom is sometimes, sometimes ... well, anyway, I decide about me. See, I trust myself. I do. I didn't used to, but I'm starting to more lately. With things like s-e-x, I know there's more. It's having a baby. Oh, believe me, Aunt Sue, I'm not planning a baby. I'm just curious. I want to know stuff. It's interesting. Mom would just freak out if I tried to ask her questions. And Dad, he's, well, he's a dad. I wanted to ask a woman. Don't worry, I'm kinda on a fact-finding mission."

"Well, good, I feel better. I guess. Anyway, Maclyn, you certainly have a very mature attitude about it all for an 11-year-old girl – "

"Nearly 13," I interrupted again.

"Yes, of course, nearly 13." She smiled and hugged me for longer than I can remember being hugged.

Once Aunt Sue left my room, I realized I didn't need to talk with her after all. When it comes right down to it, a girl knows what she wants. And she knows what's right for her.

It's that intuition; that little voice inside her head, inside her heart that says just what to do.

Babies at 12, really ... Why can't a girl just want to *know* stuff and not *do* stuff? Really.

19

ERIC, THE THOUGHTFUL BROTHER

I keep regretting all the missed talks I could've had with Grandpa. I wish we'd had more like the time in the hospital. Could be Grandpa was just waiting for the right moment. Because if he had shared all those ideas with me before, there wouldn't have been anything important to say on his deathbed.

I had never spoken before to Grandpa about my own thoughts of God, Goddess. How did he know to pick me? Maybe he had tried talking to Kenny or Marc on these subjects but could see they just didn't understand. He should've talked to Eric. Like I said, Grandpa never really got on with him.

Funny, though, Grandpa didn't seem as afraid as I'd imagine I'd be, waiting to die. The idea now, at 13, scares me like nothing else. What frightens me more, though, is someone close dying, like Mom or Dad or Pais or Eric.

A few months ago, on my 13th birthday, just weeks before Grandpa died, Eric shared some ideas on life with me. I guess he was worried about me growing up too fast without understanding what Life's all about. Not that he had all the answers for me; he just wanted to head me off in the right direction.

October 31, 1978, my 13th birthday, home

"Happy Birthday, Sis, you old lady!" Eric bounded into my bedroom. Having recently turned 20, no longer a teen, he considered himself an official adult with adult privileges - namely giving advice to kids. More importantly, Eric felt a synergy with me, his leaving teendom the same year I entered it. Two disparate steps into a wide-open future, one neither of us realized would soon take an unforeseen twist.

We had all just finished birthday dinner (Spinach Lasagna, garlic bread, salad dressed with Thousand Island) and birthday cake (a bubble-gum ice cream one with white icing and a pink rose from 31 Flavors) and opening birthday presents (Styx new album *Pieces of Eight* from Marc and Kevin, a piece of paper from Dad promising to take me to see *Superman*, a denim shirt with lots of embroidery stitched all over and colorful toe socks from Mom, and a gold floating heart necklace from everyone).

Before dinner, I'd slipped into my Halloween costume and walked over to Paisley's house to pass out leaflets. When I returned home for the celebrations, Eric told me he wanted to deliver my present in private, after all the family stuff. But when he entered my room, his hands were empty.

"I thought you were coming here to give me my birthday present."

"Well, I am. It's just not maybe something you were expecting. See, all this birthday celebration stuff, Eliza, I just don't think it's always worthy of a present, something you buy and wrap to be unwrapped. I'd rather just have a kind of special talk, to explain to you ... for you to understand ... to ..."

I looked up blankly then back down at my toe socks, trying to decide if I like the pink on the pinky toe or the purple on the big toe. "Have I done something to annoy you, Eric?" I slowly returned my gaze back to him.

"Just listen for a moment. Okay?" I sat attentively on the

edge of my bed. He stood before me, looking a bit like Johnny Cash in his usual black attire: black turtle neck, black Levi's, black ankle boots. He cleared his throat, "See Sis, for this one day of the year there's this love and joy."

"Yeah, but isn't this all a good thing, just this one day?"

"Sure, it's a good thing. Birthdays are fun. It's a good thing seeing everyone together and all - that's great. But, shouldn't it be that way all year round?"

"I guess." I wondered where this conversation was headed. My toe socks were distracting me to no end. Eric better move it along.

He paused, seemed frustrated. I could tell because whenever Eric didn't know what to say, he'd stick out his lower jaw and bite his top lip (sort of like Paisley). He looked so funny, like an ape, especially since he had gotten his hair cut so short. Those big black eyes shone even more. I had to suppress a giggle.

"The point is, this is your birthday, and I wanted to give you something special, something that you won't outgrow, or lose, or break because your 13th birthday is so important for you. I thought the best thing I could give you would be some advice."

Oh no, I thought to myself, this is going to be one of Eric's telling me what to do, what's right (his way) and what's wrong (that would be everyone else's ways). Mostly, I loved listening to Eric but only when he discussed things with me not lectured. I guessed this time wasn't going to be so preachy, and being 13, I felt more compelled to listen, to show I was growing up.

I stopped twisting the loose red thread from my right toe sock, put my hands in my lap, and gave Eric the attention he commanded, the attention he deserved. Always a rather thoughtful person, tonight he seemed especially serious.

"I know you think I'm always telling you what to do and giving you advice. You think I'm a know-it-all." He smiled at me confident I sat in full agreement. He then started pacing up and down the room, stopping now and again to put his thin hands earnestly upon his Levi-covered hips to say something. "It's like this, Eliza. I love you all year round, not just on your birthday." I smiled. "And I think that giving you a present on this one day is, well, kind of superficial, you know, kind of phony."

"You know you don't need a reason to give me a present, Eric," I joked.

"Come on, you know what I mean. See, I love you everyday of the year. I'm proud of you all the time and will always be proud of you no matter what you do, no matter what you say, for the rest of your life," he paused then added as an afterthought, "no matter what you become. And I hope you will feel that way about me, always, and about the rest of the family, too.

"But, Mom and Dad, they may not always be proud of you. You see the way they get angry with me for my lifestyle, my beliefs, because I decided to be a Buddhist? Mom's always grumbling how she doesn't know why I did it. She doesn't know what to do for Christmas, or even New Year's. She makes it all about her. Even though they pretend to let it be okay for us to make our own choices, I think deep down they are hoping we choose to be just like them. It's like our choosing something different means we think we're better, but that's just not true. We are thinking on our own. I'm sure you've noticed how Dad always says, 'as long as you're happy,' but you still feel like you need to do things his way. You'll probably never really be what they want. You need to just be what you want and know that everything will work out just fine."

"But Dad does say I should be whatever I want. He says he'll love me no matter what I choose." Rushing to my dad's defense, I felt a tremendous sense of protection spread through me as if I'd come under attack. Suddenly, Eric seemed the stranger.

"What Dad says and what he feels are two different things. Remember the time you and Paisley formed that little political group and Dad kept saying he wanted you to experience different ideas, yet when he learned about your group he got really angry?"

I nodded, noting my family's unawareness of my continuation in the organization. Oddly, they observed nothing when I left the house tonight to distribute leaflets with Paisley to trick-or-treaters. Okay, so maybe Eric knows something here about Dad. "Yeah, I think I know what you mean, Eric. Like that time I wanted to get a new puppy after Snoopy died. And Dad said that if it would make me happy, I could have another one. Then I found Alfie, that little stray, remember, wandering down the street, and I brought him home and Dad and Mom got really angry because he was so dirty, but really, I never understood why he wouldn't let me keep him. Yeah, I see that. It's those contradictions Paisley was talking to me about."

"Yeah, but you know, Mom and Dad do want you to be happy, I really believe that, but on their terms. And, just as you get older and will maybe go to college, what you'll want to study may not be what they'll want you to study. You might choose a way of life that doesn't quite live up to their ideas of you. This is the present I wanted to give you, to sort of prepare you to trust yourself, think for yourself. You're 13 now, that sort of steppingstone age towards independent thinking. It could be like a new beginning for you, or at least a time when you begin to assess your life, think about why you are here, what's your purpose."

He stared intently at me, those large dark eyes seeing inside me, searching for my knowing, waiting for signs that I understood. Then his gaze moved, not his head, not even his eyes, but the intensity softened as if he turned in upon himself, searching within his mind, heart, for words, the right words, truthful words. He continued.

"I made the mistake of simply rebelling. Everything they – Mom and Dad – wanted I went against. I've learned now that rebelling isn't the answer. Talking is. If you can learn this, you might keep yourself from separating from them like I have."

At 15, Eric ran away from home to join a group of kids in L.A. I guess they were a kind of religious group. I was only ten at the time, so I didn't really get it all, and no one really told me anything. What I do remember is the feeling, a feeling of insecurity, of not knowing where my brother was or when he'd be back. And the way Mom and Dad talked, I believed he had done something really evil.

Would Eric be brainwashed into killing people, write bloody warnings on rich people's mansions? It was 1973, just after all the Charles Manson Family stuff, and I had sneaked enough peeks of the evening news to be scared that my brother might end up a cell-mate of the crazed looking bearded man. My worries didn't subside until ten months later when Eric strolled through the front door, a bit thinner, a baldhead, and, he told me later, "a bit wiser".

He had left a note the night he ran off and had written often while away. But Dad never wrote him, even though he'd often say how much he wished Eric would just come home. Three years later, anyone can see their relationship is not the same. Dad hardly talks to Eric.

"Eric, I don't want to do something that'll make Dad or Mom stop talking to me, but I do want to make my own decisions. What should I do when they don't want me to do something that I know is okay?"

"Hmm, well, I guess, from my experience, I'd say you'll need to tell Dad what he wants to hear then do your thing on the sly." That was one of the few times I'd heard Eric make a joke and seen him laugh, really laugh. "No, really, you should just do what you think's best but be aware of the consequences."

"Like Mom and Dad grounding me or something?"

"Yeah. You know I don't want you doing what I say simply because I'm suggesting these things. I want you to think about them. I like how you decided it's wrong to eat meat. That's cool. You should decide things on your own at your own pace. Don't let Mom and Dad force their opinions on you." He stopped, smiled, and let out a little chuckle. "And don't let me either. Don't try to fit into the role they want you to play or one anyone else wants you to play. You need to just appreciate Mom and Dad's views, so that, maybe, they will appreciate yours.

"They are set in their ways, so it's difficult for them to see yours. I hope you're listening to me, Sis, and trying to understand what I'm saying." And then he stopped. During his long speech, he had nestled himself on the floor, leaning against the wall between my desk and dresser, sort of cocooned himself into a corner. By the end of his speech, he had curled his legs up into himself, wrapping his arms around them, and resting his head on top of his knees. I thought, there's Eric when he was eight. I know it. I bet that is exactly what he used to do.

I smiled, "I am listening, Eric, to every single word. But I think I'll need more time to think about all this. Maybe we can have more talks, special ones, not just on my birthday. You know, kind of how you said we shouldn't just give presents on someone's birthday, do it whenever you feel."

"Yeah, that's good. Hey, how about we go up to Pinecone Pond and listen for owls?"

"That sounds good."

We slipped on our coats, and Eric snuggly positioned his navy blue dockworker's cap on top his half-bald head. We drove up to the moonlit pond with Kansas' "Dust in the Wind" playing on the radio.

While walking along the bank and listening for owls, Eric told me he was thinking of going to India to visit some temples. However, he said, he probably wouldn't go until next summer. I told him that I hoped he did get to go; but inside, I was crying, sobbing, praying that something would keep him near me, forever.

It was a rather spooky night by the water. The end of October brings cooler evenings and sudden gusty winds. Plus, it was Halloween Night, which only added to the eerie sadness of a deserted mountain pond and the possibility of my favorite brother leaving home.

A nearly full moon cast a luminous glow over the still dark waters reflecting the scant clouds upon the glassy surface. A winter chill blew up from the darkness. Yet as I walked with my brother, I felt the warmth like a blanket wrap across my shoulders.

We returned around 11. Dad sat in front of the television, ready to watch the late news. I walked over to him, kissed his soft forehead, and headed up to bed. Just as I was about to turn out my light, a knock sounded at the door.

"Come in."

"Sorry, it's just me, again." Eric half-entered. "Hey, Eliza, don't tell Mom and Dad about India yet. Okay?"

"Yeah, sure," I agreed, feeling that pang in my heart again. "My lips are sealed." I turned the invisible key on my lips.

"Thanks. G'night, Old Lady," he joked, chuckled a bit, and closed the door.

As I turned on my new Styx album, I realized how completely different all my brothers were. Sure, Kenny was the oldest, but he wasn't the wisest.

One thing was clear. No one had ever given me a better gift than Eric's wise words the night I turned 13.

20

RUMORS, SUZY ALLISON, AND THE HANDBALL WALL

Young minds are impressionable. I should know, I have one and it's full of indentations. Grandpa once told me that as you get older, Life enlarges and focuses, like a telescope that nears the moon, seeing more of the intricacies, the craters, the imperfections, and the beauty. Like a camera on zoom. Instead of simple four-by-five Polaroids of the world, you can focus, use the wide-angle lenses, filters, tri-pods, and adjust the lighting. He said the world falls into view in a way you'd never expect.

Grandpa must've been a great teacher for Mom. She's never really talked about it, though. When she gets home, I'm adding that to my list – learn more about Grandpa.

I guess our families teach us just as much as school. While we're growing up, everything affects who we will be. Like a shirt that's torn or soiled, no matter how hard you work to repair it there will always be a crooked stitch or ghost stain. So we should be careful when the shirt is new and clean.

This isn't something kids ponder much. Kids tend to do then think – if at all. That's how all that gossipy stuff gets started. Like Suzy Allison. Oh, haven't I told you? Well, it just happened.

The rumor.

January 3, 1979 (today), age 13, school

Okay, so you've heard of the old sex ed class? Either you've had it, are anticipating it, dreading it, or could care less (doubtful; but I'll believe you).

Well, we had films and "discussions" in sixth grade. Last year, the nurse came in to talk to us. This year, even though we are studying chemicals and stuff in science, Mr. Finley told us we would be having a "Family Life Seminar". Just for three days this week. Today was our first session. We had to turn in permission slips. Dad signed mine, didn't even read it. Good, didn't really want to talk with him about it anyway.

As far as I know, only one student's dad - a Father actually - wouldn't sign the slip. Suzy Allison. Mr. Finley sent her to the library. She didn't seem to mind at all.

Here's the rumor.

Lisa Mitchell said Suzy got all the info she needed in sixth grade (the last time, she spent sex-ed in the library). She acquired just about everything, apparently, according to Lisa, from Bobby Thompson, and Randy Miles, and Joe Basketball (which pains me).

You know how rumors fly around school. Some have their own wings, and some get a jet-propelled boost from jealous classmates.

"I heard she took turns behind the handball wall with them," Lisa shared with me at lunch today. As she unwrapped the cellophane from her PB&J, she shook her head. "Of course, who'd be surprised about Suzy? Remember second grade when she walked right through the boys' kickball game and straight up to Bobby Thompson and just planted one right on his mouth? Remember?"

Who didn't? I bit into my apple and chewed thoughtfully. I knew I shouldn't be listening to this, but I couldn't help it. "Yeah. But do you remember Bobby's reaction?"

Lisa laughed. "I know, well, everyone knew what Suzy wanted. But Bobby was disgusted."

Now we both giggled. See, this was not something I could talk about with Paisley. In fact, if she'd walked up, *she'd* be disgusted.

"Not in sixth grade," I added. "He didn't look so grossed out with Suzy behind the handball wall then."

School just doesn't interest Suzy. It never really has. But most teachers don't notice. She's polite in class. Sits up. Pays attention. Listens. Raises her hand every other day. (Seriously, I checked this out. She's worked out some plan that if she raises her hand every other day to answer some really easy question, or even sometimes just ask one, she never gets called on. Now, I call that pretty smart.)

Of course, she always sits up front. Every kid knows the front row is either where the bad kids sit so the teacher can keep her eye on you, or where the good kids sit so they can kiss up to the teacher.

Suzy is not a bad kid. In fact, I kind of admire her. She's really quite pretty, too. Her long black hair always so neatly tied up in a lace ribbon, sometimes braided. Her clothes neatly pressed, but often just a might too small, so that when she sits down, her pants fall a little low, low enough for nearly every boy to sit up straight for a peak. Still, Suzy has a grace. Even in fifth grade.

"How does she get away with it?" I asked Lisa. "Look at her today when Mr. Finley excused her to the library. She just gathered her books and walked right through the rows to the back door. Not embarrassed. And every boy watched her." Even Joe Basketball, I whined inside. Her billowy sleeves brushed each boy, and her slight lip-glossed smile caught each eye. The shy boys blushed and the tough ones nodded.

After she exited, the scent of *Gee Your Hair Smells Terrific* filled the room. It smelled like summer.

"I guess you learn what you need to learn somehow," Lisa interrupted my thoughts. "Besides, who'd want to tell

Reverend Allison they were pregnant?"

We both shuddered a bit. I mulled over the oddity of getting pregnant while still in school. The thing is if you got pregnant, you couldn't go to school. Now, there's a ridiculous rule: let's keep out the kids who really need help, that'll teach 'em.

The lunch bell rang and we scooped up our trash and half-eaten sandwiches and apples. I scanned the lunchroom for Joe Basketball. Why was he invading my thoughts so much these days?

No Joe; but there was Suzy. A burn traveled up my face. I glanced quickly to the floor, noting the dirty napkins and other trash strewn all over. I half-expected to see my own face, my own gossipy little face. Suzy didn't deserve our whispers. She didn't actually do anything wrong.

Unfortunately, it's girls like Suzy who get talked about. Girls who are pretty. Girls who the boys like so easily. Girls who smell like summer.

Girls like me have a lot to learn from girls like Suzy Allison. What I might not realize is that Suzy could learn a thing or two from Eliza Mills.

21

THE ADMITTANCE OF LISA MITCHELL

I suppose I can't really just toss in my talk with Lisa today without telling you how I met her. That wouldn't be fair. I wouldn't want you to get the wrong impression of her either. She's not a gossip, really. She's pretty smart. She's probably the only girl who's ever really challenged Paisley.

In fact, it was nearly a year ago today.

January 1, 1978, age 12, Parks' home

Heavy rains fell steadily all that New Year's Day. We had two interviews for the organization. Paisley impatiently tapped her pencil as we waited for Lisa Mitchell. I could tell that Pais was ready for a challenge. She surely had already formed her opinion. She only agreed to interview her because I had asked.

Lisa entered Paisley's room wearing an expensive looking hooded navy blue down jacket with the ski-lift ticket status symbol still dangling from last season's runs, ironed denims with a crease down each leg (who irons their jeans?), a soft pink sweater, faux fur-lined boots, and a nervous braces-free-perfectly-straight smile. Her long brown hair, thick-lashed green eyes and pimple-free complexion set her in line as some movie star's daughter, but in reality her father owned a construction company and lots and lots of undeveloped desert land. Mr. Mitchell, the typical American rags-to-riches story.

"Has your dad ever owned cattle," Pais wasted no time. Her question shot out sharply in drill-sergeant style.

"Cattle?" repeated Lisa who slid off her jacket, sat down on the blue shag carpet. She raised her eyebrows followed by some squinting and a little lip biting, clearly wondering what she had gotten herself into. "Well, um, no, um, not that I know of. He owns a bunch of land out in Las Palimas, that's all. He builds houses here in Santa Nina, some buildings, too. But do you mean like does he have farm land?" She stopped talking, bit her left bottom lip, pushing the right side out and up, then sucked the whole lip in, relaxed and sighed, "Why are you asking me about my dad? He's not joining your club. I am."

Uh oh, things weren't looking good for Lisa. First, she turned the questioning to Paisley. Second, she used the c-word. Paisley had a real thing about that word. She said it sounded like some ladies group that met for tea and facials. An organization, on the other hand, sounded serious, like it meant business. And Paisley Park meant business.

"Okay, now, we're not a *club*," heavy emphasis on the b "we're an or-gan-ni-za-shun, right? And, um, could you just answer my questions? If we let you in, then you can ask *us* some questions, okay?" Paisley glanced over at me, raised her left eyebrow as if to say, *what do you think here, should I continue?*

I took this rare moment of hesitant Paisley to speak, "Lisa, you're a vegetarian, right?"

"Yeah."

Paisley continued, "Well, why?"

"For your same reasons, I guess. It's just not right to kill animals for food or clothes or anything like that when we don't need to. That's why I don't wear leather, not even my belt, see, it's that fake suede-like stuff. Even my boots are man-made. She uncrossed her legs and flexed her right foot in the air a bit, proudly displaying the boot's sole and the markings ALL MAN-MADE MATERIALS.

"Good," Paisley made a note on her pad.

Amy and Heather, who sat up on bended knees, smiled encouragingly at Lisa, then looked over to Paisley, probably beginning to think this girl was a bit nuts. Still, they made no motion to leave or interrupt. You see, Paisley possessed this sort of power, a charm that captivated people. Her serious, matter-of-fact ways kept others intrigued.

It was as if Paisley knew something we didn't, so we wanted to hang around to find out what that was. We hoped in some way that her charm would seep out onto us, so we, too, could leave others wondering.

Suddenly, Lisa broke out, "I just don't think we have the right. To kill them. It's really cruel, you know. It's wrong, that's all, just wrong. I try to explain that to my parents, but they don't get it. My mom worries that I'm not eating right. But I read that spinach has lots of iron, so I eat that all the time.

"When they have steak, I ask for extra spinach. When they have pork chops, I ask for extra spinach. You know, they can't force us."

Good answer, Lisa, I thought. Pais would like that one. And sure enough, as she bent her head down to write on her pad, I spied a little smile curling up on my high-minded friend's serious face. Then Paisley moved the interview onto more thought-provoking subjects.

Government. "I want to vote when I'm 18, for sure. But for now, I just listen to as much news as I can. I like hearing about the world."

Integration. "My little brother was bussed to a school across town last year. He made a really good friend, Gerardo. But now that they stopped the bussing, he's back at Parkview. So once in awhile, Gerardo's mom brings him over. He's a cool kid, but I can tell he's a little unsure of our house." (Who wouldn't be; where most of us have a swing-set in the backyard, the Mitchell's have stables.) "So I think integration is a good thing because, otherwise, Tommy wouldn't have met Gerardo. We'd all just be in our little corners. That's not good."

Women working. "I'm going to be a lawyer. My mom works for the DA, so I've visited the office a few times. The DA said next summer I could work there, filing papers or something. Law's exciting. You get to hear all the gossip, but you also get to help people. I want to work for women and kids' issues, like family law or something. Well, and of course, I want to have a family."

The 70s "I'm going to have it all" girl's answer.

School. "I'm going to run for class president in ninth grade when we get to high school. I want to get them to have vegetarian lunches."

Score one big one there for Lisa.

Mr. Wicks, the principal. "Ooh, he's kind of cute, don't you think?" *Yikes, foul buzzer*! "I mean, well, he is. I'm on the newspaper, so I interviewed him last week about the new lunch schedule. Kids have been complaining that it takes too long to get your lunch. He's actually looking into changing it. Isn't that cool?"

Paisley wrote furiously then sat up and stretched her back, put her pen down and turned her neck this way and that. "Okay, well, that's good." Then she picked up her pen and tapped it against her chin, which meant another question was forming.

Lisa re-crossed her legs and folded her hands under her chin, resting her elbows on her knees, looking ready to answer anything. Pais had to admit that money didn't equal ignorance. This was an important moment for Paisley, and she needed to take it in. "Okay, last question."

All right, this was it, something good. "What's your favorite subject?"

Huh?

"Um, in school?" Lisa asked, stunned at this simple

question as the rest of us.

"Yeah, in school."

"Well, I guess," Lisa paused, stalled, obviously expecting something deeper. She stroked the soft fake fur that spilled over her man-made boots. "I guess I'd have to say math. Yeah, math."

"Math?" Paisley sounded a bit disappointed. "Do you think that is the most important thing we can learn in school that will really help us later in Life?"

Uh oh.

"You didn't say most important, you said favorite." She's got you there, Pais, I thought as I glanced over at her. Curiously, Paisley smiled, then let out a small laugh through her nose, more a burst of air, actually, than a laugh. We all giggled, relieved.

Lisa took this cue and continued, "Well, I'd still say math. It teaches us how to think, how to think quickly, how to use all of our brainpower. It teaches us to be efficient with our thoughts." Okay, now that sounded so much like Paisley, just without the math part, but everything else was pure Paisley thinking.

Lisa paused, took a breath, clearly awaiting Paisley's interruption; not hearing one, she proceeded, "You know those story problems we do in class that ask us to find out when the train will arrive by knowing how far it must travel and at what speed it's going? Well, I think that's really helpful. Being able to understand a situation with only a few pieces of information, that's useful. Kind of like Life."

"Okay then, and what about Life? What about Life-after-death, what do you think about after we die?"

This was the kind of interruption Lisa was expecting, so in a way she was prepared for it. "Life-after-death, hmmm. Well, I guess that's just something we don't really know so much about. I mean, we're living, so we can't really know about what comes after it, right?"

"I was more thinking about what you were saying about math, about how it can help us understand different situations. Can it help us understand what happens after we die?"

Give her a break, Paisley! Come on, Lisa has answered your questions for 30 minutes now, and they've been good answers, too.

The silent room breathed only in anticipation. Heather followed a tiny black crawly creature the size of a pea with hundreds of little hairy legs wriggling in the air, as it had somehow tipped over on its back.

Amy sat staring at its silent struggle. Then Lisa looked over at Pais, and we all looked back at Heather who finally flipped over the little bug with her pinky and, suddenly aware of our stares, looked up with embarrassment like a child caught staring too long through her neighbor's open window.

Lisa broke the silence. "If anyone has been there and back, they haven't been able to remember enough to tell anyone about it, so I just guess we will all have to wait until we die. You know, and, and as far as math is concerned, well, it could be quite useful in this because math and science are related. Remember Mr. Finley told us that. He said that 'every scientist is first a mathematician and every mathematician uses the scientific method when solving big problems'."

"Observation is the key, kids, to math, science and to Life!" we all chimed in, repeating our sinister science teacher's favorite phrase. Then we giggled like the schoolgirls we were.

"But, really," Lisa continued, now on a roll, "Only God can help us when we die, I think. Anyway, I'd still say math's my favorite subject, and that it's important while we're on earth." She rested her case.

Paisley stood up, walked slowly over to the window that looked out onto her backyard then leaned against the wall and stared outside as if expecting to see something. Lisa fidgeted nervously with her boot fur, a habit that was quickly beginning to annoy me. Pais turned toward her.

"Okay. Thanks for coming. We'll see you in school tomorrow."

Lisa's face paled, every drop of blood drained away, and she asked in a panic, "Is that it? You don't want me?"

I don't think any of us had realized how much Lisa wanted in the group.

"No, it's just that we all need to vote. We'll tell you at lunch tomorrow. Okay?"

Lisa blinked her eyes and released a great sigh of relief as the blood returned to her olive complexion. She put on her heavy down jacket and Pais walked her to the door.

Of course, the four of us voted her in that day. And even though Paisley didn't like having a rich girl in the organization, she admitted to liking Lisa a lot. Said she was quick and smart. Not something Paisley easily admits about others.

"You know, Eliza," Pais confided in me after we'd voted and Amy and Heather had gone home, "even though Lisa didn't seem to think about all the same things we did, or at least not as much, she didn't tell me I was wrong. And she didn't change how she felt about things. She stuck to what she believed. There's something we can learn from that. She's cool."

Sticking to your beliefs. Yeah. There is something definitely to learn there. Now, if I could only be clear on what my beliefs are, I'd have a chance at sticking to them. I knew it just meant more time thinking and listening to those voices. Believe in the voices. Hear your beliefs.

Sounds crazy and true all at once.

22

METLING WITH MAYA ANGELOU

Mom flies home tomorrow, the 5th. I can't wait. I have a whole list of things to talk to her about. More stories about Grandpa. Gossiping. Boys.

Today's history class began with talk on busing and integration. Somehow, the period ended with me thinking about boys and poetry. Busing stopped in our town two years ago. I always want to ask Shelley what she thinks about it, but it just never comes up in conversation.

Shelley Newman was our last member voted in. We interviewed her that same New Year's Day, just an hour after Lisa. I suppose what Paisley mostly liked about Shelley was simply Shelley herself.

Shelley's black. She's our only black member. In fact, I can count on my hand the number of black girls in the eighth grade. Santa Nina isn't the hotbed of multicultural variety. And, really, I don't think I ever paid much attention to color when I was little. Now with busing, I'm sort of awake to it all and see that the *world* pays attention to color.

Today, January 4, 1979, age 13 and growing, school

A friend's honesty is way more important to me than her skin color or what she eats for dinner. Still, the 70s in

California has been all about color – integration, busing, and tolerance. We've had class discussions about race in history. In Junior High we "discuss". In High School, kids debate, write research papers and join clubs declaring opinions out loud. Wow, one minute you are sitting in the cafeteria with a bunch of kids, laughing, eating, throwing food and copying homework. And the next minute, you are supposed to decide if you want to be a Future Business Leader of America or a member of the Key Club.

Shelley, my tall dark curly-haired friend, she's another story. Pais and I have known her since second grade. We used to play on the swings, team up in dodge ball, share pencils and stuff. I like having Shelley as a friend. Her dad's a fireman like mine, but they work at different stations. Both are captains, but Mr. Newman is nearly 60 and ready to retire. Shelley has one older sister and two little brothers. Her sister is seven years older, about the same age as Kenny.

Still, Mrs. Newman looks way too young to have a 20-year-old. She's tall, slender and wears the coolest sunglasses. She reminds me of Jackie O a bit. She works in the fire department's dispatch. That would be such a cool job because you get to hear about all the emergencies and help people who are panicked. I bet she's really good at that.

Shelley's a lot like her mom - really good whenever I'm all freaked out about a test or something. She always says stuff like, "Mac, you're smart. Don't worry. We studied, right? So, we're gonna do fine. Anyway, it's just a test, no big deal."

I love her laid back easy-going nature – such a contrast to Paisley who would be stressing way more than me. She's always concerned that there will be all this stuff on a test that we never studied, stuff the teacher thinks is important but wasn't in our book. I think Paisley just doesn't trust adults.

But Pais and I agree on one thing - Shelley speaks in poetry.

"Want to hear another limerick," Shelley whispered to me in Ms. Eben's third period English class today.

As Ms. Eben took attendance, her large gold-hooped earrings dangled from her head like parrot perches. Two boys' voices arose from the corner. Without flinching, she turned to Randy Miles and Roger Thomas and announced in her characteristic quiet manner, "Have a seat now, boys." They made little attempt to stop their debate over basketball stats or some other sport mumbo-jumbo.

Randy slowly moved toward his seat but apparently not quick enough for Ms. Eben. So she gradually made her way toward him as her multi-colored skirt swished against her skinny legs.

Eyes fixed on his, a smile across her face, Randy backed carefully into his seat, a broad smile on his own face and not a word from his lips.

That's all it takes – the teacher look. Ms. Eben had it down cold. Her point made, she motioned to Roger to pass out our new novels, returning to her task as though nothing had happened. Some subtle form of respect lurks within this process. Her refusal to call out a name says, *Hey, don't disrupt my class, anyone, whoever you are, I don't care. Just listen. Everyone.*

Roger picked up a stack of "I Know Why the Caged Bird Sings". He began dropping them from desk to desk. Most kids were doodling in their notebooks, talking to their neighbor, or, if you were Suzy Allison, reapplying lip-gloss.

I glanced over two rows at Joe Basketball. Sigh. How I can keep my mind on English when he's so close, I just don't know. You've got your work cut out, Ms. Eben.

"Hey, Dream Girl, anyone home?"

Shelley. Right. The limerick. "Yeah, let me see." I really loved Shelley's poetry. She handed me her notebook, the pink one, the one she kept for creative stuff. Its cover plastered with everything from people's signatures to phone numbers to math equations to peace signs. I flipped it open and found the newest Shelley creation.

This one was about our science teacher, Mr. Finley.

There was once a bald-headed teacher
Who dissected pigs and small creatures.
His lectures were a bore,
So we'd stare at the door;
Rather than at his swine-like features.

I giggled and maybe even snorted a bit. Pulling my hand quickly to my mouth, I started to return the notebook. A hand darted out grabbing the book. I stopped. It was Randy Miles.

"What's this, some more gossip? Lemme see."

"Hey," Shelley tried to grab the book, "That's mine. Give it back."

"Hang on. Let me just have a little read." Randy Miles, Mr. Know-it-All, ran his blue eyes over the poem, let out a smirk and tossed the book on Shelley's desk. "Is that Finley? Yeah, he's a pig. Those ears, Man. They look like Spock, don't ya think? Pug nose, too. Good one, Shell."

Shelley took in the compliment as Roger dropped a novel in front of her.

Wait, what was that? Did Shelley just smile at Roger? I glanced back as the skinny kid continued flinging books down. Roger turned again toward my poetic friend for a moment. Her attention had since moved to the book's cover.

A black bird flew across a red sky, upward toward the title.

"It's pretty, huh?" I asked Shelley, trying to strike up conversation, hoping to redirect it toward Roger, but she surprised me and I forgot my original intent.

"Yeah. My mom told me about it all ready. It's gonna be sad, but then it will lift our spirits." Shelley smiled at me. "Life does that, you know, gives us pain so we need to find a way to rise up out of it all. Otherwise, we just go along day to day and never think we need lifting."

Deep words from my corny friend. I looked back at my book, flipped open the pages and stopped at a line: "... giggles hung in the air like melting clouds..."

"Wow, this Miss Angelou, she can write," I offered to Shelley. Look here, and I pointed to the page.

Shelley read it, smiled. "This is gonna be good."

Ms. Eben pulled in our attention with a throat clearing, and we turned toward our favorite English teacher. Everyone except for Roger Thomas who I noted out of the corner of my left eye was staring straight at my friend Shelley Newman.

I grinned in triumph. I was right. Love hung in the air like sweet dewdrops. Then Ms. Eben's voice broke into my thoughts like a jewel thief.

"This is not a love story, kids," she smiled, reading our minds a little too closely. "This is real. This happened. Maya Angelou survived terrible events during a difficult time in our history. She never sat around English class like you all, laughing, whispering, fixing her make-up (several faces turned toward Suzy). Maya Angelou witnessed and experienced things I hope none of you will ever know."

Silence. Eyes forward. I had to check that I was actually breathing. "Are you ready to hear an amazing, courageous, painful story?"

We stared, some nodded. Randy spat out, "I'm ready!" We laughed, pleased he broke the tension.

"There'll be some funny stuff, too, but you'll need to pay attention. Maya Angelou's a poet, so she writes with lyricism, with style. She constructs sentences with words in the way a sculptor models lumps of clay into museum-worthy statues. Listen to the story, notice the words, learn what you can. Maya Angelou writes from experience, but that doesn't mean you will need to go through these hardships to someday be good writers. You will, though, need to pay attention to the poetry in your own lives. That's what Miss Angelou does. Ready?"

Shelley, Roger, Paisley, and everyone sat up and prepared to listen.

I settled in my chair as Ms. Eben started to read. Okay, Maya, show me what you've got.

After what seemed seconds, Ms. Eben was collecting and counting the books. They stay in school, she said. She wants us to read the story together. I don't care. I'm going to the library after school tomorrow and checking out the Caged Bird.

You can't put a schedule on poetry.

My life isn't melting; it's solidifying, forming into some sort of real sculpture from my experiences, from the poetic moments of my time here on earth.

I suppose Maya Angelou is now a part of that.

23

PAISLEY'S GOT IT, BUT I DON'T

Friday, January 5, 1979, age 13, home

Mom flies home tonight. I can't wait. Like I said, it's often not until something or someone is gone that you realize you like having them around. I miss having another girl in the house, too.

Last night, I overheard Dad talking to her on the phone. Something is strange. I thought I heard Dad say, "Where will we put that?" I wondered, put what? For some reason, I imagined this that to be big, really big. Why else would you wonder where to put it? If it's small, you don't worry. It will go somewhere. If it's big, big like a bed, or big like a horse, then you wonder, where will we put that?

Dad asked us to do a good cleaning for Mom. That pretty much meant the boys would clean up their rooms and I would clean up the house. That's okay; just vacuuming and dishes and stuff. It makes me laugh, really. My big brothers. Older. Messier. Takes a little sister to keep things tidy.

I think a little vacuuming might calm my nerves from today's lecture ala Paisley Park. Topic? Careers.

Earlier today, walking home

Brrrinnggg!! We hurried out the front doors avoiding tiny seventh graders and bulging backpacks. Pais and I walked home everyday. We didn't even need to plan it, we just knew; even though I had P.E. sixth period and she had math. Right after that final bell rang, we would instinctively head to our lockers and toward the outer doors. We were so in-sync that neither one of us needed to look for the other. There she was. Then us. Stepping down the front steps in unison, reaching the sidewalk at precisely the same moment, turning toward home, sharing our day, without a breath or heartbeat out of rhythm.

By the time we reached Paisley's house, I felt like hanging out for a bit before heading in for the Big Clean. Wish we had a housekeeper, I thought. Maybe one day I could own my own cleaning business. I feel like I manage one already with my crazy brothers.

Once inside the Parks, however, it was all about food. We both entered through the front door like two sisters returning home. I had a key to their house but never needed it since they kept their door unlocked all day.

After raiding the kitchen for Oreos, milk and corn nuts, we settled in the living room to start our homework. You could hear the silence. With Bob at work and Linda likely at one of her gazillion volunteer jobs, the Park's house seemed to absorb the quiet.

Where was John F? I wondered.

Paisley's tapping disturbed my fantasy of him walking through the front door and asking us if we wanted to go to DQ for ice cream.

While sitting in her living room reading a history lesson on the Industrial Revolution, Paisley rhythmically tapped her pencil against the armrest. She sat in her father's plush brown corduroy LaZy Boy recliner. However, Pais didn't recline, instead choosing to sit upright, legs curled underneath, book nestled across her lap and the armrest, her right hand tapping the pencil in staccato.

I chose to spread belly down across their worn multi-colored soft sofa. My gangly teenage legs extending over one end while my book rested up against the other. My eyes sleepily read about "major shifts in technological, socioeconomic and cultural conditions, blah, blah, Western countries, blah, process known as industrialization, blah, blah ..."

"I wonder if these inventors made a lot of money?" Paisley's question interrupted my boredom.

"I suppose so."

"Is that all you have to say? Come on, Eliza," Pais said and rolled her eyes. "I doubt I will ever invent something - like an object - maybe a new way of living, though. I think I might invent an idea."

Now I rolled my eyes, "What do you mean, 'an idea'?"

"Well, with animals. You know, like how you can live with them, not eat them. Our plan, remember?"

"Yeah, okay, but that's not really an invention." My daily hope to tell something to Paisley that she didn't already know prompted my continuous challenge of her every idea.

"Of course, that's what I just said, if you had been listening. It wouldn't be a new device or machine but a new way. It wouldn't be a new idea, really, but our organization would help bring it about. You know? Get it?"

"Um, kind of," I said, not really understanding, finding myself suddenly interested in hearing more about 19th century British textiles. So I did what I always did when Paisley took our conversations a bit too far for me, I changed the subject. "Are you going to make the organization your life, Pais? I mean, is that how you plan on making a living?"

Pais straightened her back and squinted her eyes, still tapping that pencil, but now on her lips, caught in deep thought. "I know when you don't want to talk about something, Eliza. You think you are so clever, changing the subject, but I'm not stupid. Come on, I want to figure this out, think it out more. You help me do that; so play along, will ya?"

Guilt invaded my body, forcing its way up from my gut to just below the surface of my skin, vibrating across my face, emitting a red glow around my cheeks. "Whatever," I responded, still staring at my text, rereading the same sentence I'd been reading for the last five minutes.

"I'm watching you, sister." She knew I loved when she called me that. I relaxed.

"Okay, whatever you think, but at least answer my question."

"Hey, don't you change the subject back!"

"I'm not, you are. I asked. So answer."

"Alright then. So, you want to know what I want to be when I grow up?" she mocked me, but I remained firm, this time looking her straight in the eye.

"Yeah."

"Well, I want to be a veterinarian."

"A vet? Really? And give animals shots and operate on them and deliver their babies? Oooh, yuck! That just sounds, yuck, yuck, yuck," I said with a dramatic shiver.

Paisley laughed at my squeamishness. "I just want to help animals, and if that means giving them shots and delivering babies, well, I'm not afraid of that." (Can't you hear the triumph in her voice?)

"No, I suppose you wouldn't be," I mumbled.

"What was that, Eliza? I didn't hear you," she mocked, luring me into admitting some sort of defeat, but I couldn't see what there was to be wrong about. Ugh! That guilt again, squirming up from my belly to my face.

"I thought you were going to be a child psychiatrist?" That's what she had told me last year anyway.

"No. A vet. It just makes sense. I mean, there's Artemis, such a mutt, and I love her." Ooh, the L-word. It's a rare moment when my heady friend mentions love.

The Parks don't have any other pets. Just Artemis the mongrel. Linda's allergic to cats. John F used to have a hamster and some fish, but the fish drowned and the hamster, Budweiser, Bud for short, died of cancer. Bob buried him in the backyard. That was six years ago. Artemis arrived the next summer, and guess what she dug up by their big pine tree? Fortunately, Artemis delivered her treasure to Pais, so John F never knew. She just put it in a cookie tin and re-buried it. Artemis hasn't bothered Bud since.

"I guess a vet makes sense, you're right. It's not like you ever worried about that stiff little rodent corpse," I agreed. "And, in third grade, you thought Billy Gold's snake was cool." In fact, she wanted to hold it, but Billy wouldn't let her, saying girls were meant to be afraid of snakes and shouldn't touch them. Pais just kicked Billy in the shin and told him she hoped his snake got him into a lot of trouble. It did.

"You'd probably be good at that. Helping animals. It's not like you'd save their lives then go home and have a hamburger either." Paisley's career choice didn't come as a complete surprise. It made sense - a career that combines her two passions: love for animals and love for telling people how to treat animals. "Well, it's almost like my dad saving people's lives in fires and stuff."

"Yeah, sort of." She pulled the mangled black tie from her hair and reset her ponytail. "What do you want to be, Eliza? A tree surgeon?"

"A tree surgeon?" I repeated, a little confused. "What is that supposed to mean? Someone who operates on trees? Where'd you get that from?"

"Well, you love to climb them and hang out in them, so you know, I figured, why not take care of them. Tree surgeons exist. Seriously, I'm not kidding."

"Okay, well, whatever, that's not what I want to be," desperately attempting to mask my hurt. I couldn't save my maple from Dad. I stared out the window into the Park's jungly backyard over toward my house. "I don't know what I want to be. I just don't know. Yet."

"You will. Don't worry, Eliza. Just wait. Someday you will know exactly what you want. And, it will be so clear to you, you will wonder what took you so long to realize it."

Everyday, I listen to my instincts, waiting for them to tell me what to do. I'm sure they're just waiting for the right moment; then like Pais said, it'll all be so clear.

Oh, I hope so. I really hope so.

24

DAD'S THOUGHTS AND TREE STUMPS

While at the library checking out the book Ms. Eben said not to read ahead in, I happened upon a book on trees. Paisley had planted the thought in my mind. I do like trees, so why not be a tree surgeon.

I rode home with Maya and a few varieties of maples and oaks hidden inside my beat-up blue backpack. The thought about careers stirred a gentle excitement inside me; but I wanted a little advice from Dad first. Riding home, splashing through rain puddles, I figured my fireman dad might be able to clue me in on the world of work. Problem is, he didn't speak Eliza. He spoke Dad.

Saturday, January 6, 1979, age 13, home

Tonight moved along like an ordinary quiet winter evening, the kind that doesn't feel like one night but many packed into one. Just sitting with my parents watching an old Jane Fonda movie, glancing at the clock, only five minutes, or four, since last checked; unsure why I'm even checking the time, nothing to wait for, nothing to expect or anticipate, except for the passing of time.

Dad had the day off and had spent much of it helping Mom with all her unpacking and laundry. Actually, that box of mystery that she had brought home from Uncle Bert's still sits patiently unopened. She said she isn't ready to open it, so it sits in the front hall like a tomb. Each time I stroll passed it, I put my ear up to its cold cardboard exterior, listening. I almost half-expect ticking or whimpering or some kind of movement. With no air holes visible, I've let my imagine rest. By evening, its contents seemed less interesting.

All the boys ventured out, except for Eric who remained holed up reading in the attic – as usual. Mom and Dad sat quietly in the den where I soon joined them. Just past eight, Dad had already donned his red- and blue- checkered flannel PJs and sat snug in his favorite upholstered recliner reading the newspaper. Mom had brewed a pot of hot tea, which rested boldly on the coffee table next to lemon slices and a sugar bowl. She wore her maroon housecoat that buttoned down the left side below her armpit.

Before a complete entrance into the quiet room, I quietly stood in the kitchen doorway. Mom occupied the family-favorite brown corduroy chair (Dad's next favorite after the recliner), thoughtfully picking dirt from beneath her unpolished fingernails, oblivious to the world outside. So deeply focused on this robotic chore, she appeared not to hear me as I let the saloon-like kitchen doors swing shut behind me and took my place on the cushiony brown couch.

Only Rowan politely wagged her tail in welcome a few times until I patted her soft black head allowing her to resume a dormant position. The movie had already started, 15 minutes had passed since my entry, and now a noisy amusement park commercial colorfully shouted from the screen.

Mom looked up, brushing bits of dirt from her lap. "Oh, Maclyn, I didn't hear you come in. Don't sneak around."

"Sorry, Mom, but I didn't, I wasn't sneaking. I just – ."

"Maclyn," Dad interrupted angrily. Referring to me by my

complete birth-certificate name said enough. "Don't talk back to your mother like that. Apologize."

"I did, I said – "

"Maclyn."

"Sorry, Mom," I turned toward her and squeezed out my meaningless words. "I didn't mean to scare you. Um, or talk back. Sorry."

"That's okay, Honey," she gave me one of those looks that says don't worry about Dad, I understand.

We resumed our gaze at the television. I can't quite remember the name of the movie, but it had something to do with murder and a prostitute. I'm sure if my parents had realized what we were all watching, they would have told me to leave.

My attention, however, lay elsewhere anyway. More important things occupied my mind, and I wanted to talk to Dad. That afternoon, Paisley and I were talking about careers. She's so sure of her life as a vet. I'm not so sure of anything.

Fortunately, the movie played on the mega-commercial station. I let the first few pass while I considered my questions. Then, after about 30 minutes, I broke the silence.

Knowing I had only about three minutes, I pounced. "Dad, how'd you know you wanted to be a fireman?"

"How'd I know? Well, uh, - why do you ask?"

"Just wondering, that's all. Why are you a fireman?"

"Well, it was just something I'd always wanted to be, you know. Ever since I was a little boy. I don't know, really, never stopped to ask myself that, what with all the electricity bills due, mouths to feed, just sort of became one, and now it's - what? 17? No, 20 – 20 years, yep." He paused while his eyes fixed a stare into some space just above the TV. "Didn't I ever tell you my story?" He turned to me. I shook my head.

"No, not about why you're a fireman."

"Really? I must have. When I was a little boy living in Hollywood? Really?" I shook my head again. "Hmm, must've told it a million times to the boys." Of course, I thought, it's a boy-story, so he never bothered to tell me.

He continued, apparently happy to tell it for the millionth and one time. "So once, the apartment building next to my folks' – well, you know, it was a hot muggy day, kind of like today, - and that day, anyway, the building next door caught fire. It was so big, people screaming, flames shooting out from windows and mothers hanging their babies out of those windows and screaming. The building stood about seven stories high, and the fire patrols came and just saved everyone. No one - not one single person, animal, not one baby - died. Of course, the blaze completely destroyed the building, gutted it, but everyone survived.

"The newspapers went on for months about how great our firemen were, what heroes they were, and there were plaques from the mayor, interviews on TV, people honking horns, shaking their hands. I remember just thinking, 'wow, they saved all those people'. And, I thought," Dad paused, looked up at the TV. The movie had already begun. He looked back at me and tried to continue in a hushed voice. "I thought, I want to save people and be a hero. That was my little boy dream. My dream hung on, mostly. I wanted to be that hero. Besides, I really didn't know what else I could - "

"Shh," came a finger to Mom's mouth. "Come on, let's watch the movie."

"...I could do, you know," Dad continued in a whisper, turning closer toward me. "It's not that I wasn't smart enough to be anything else, to be a professional, a doctor, or something," he caught Mom's glare. "I really felt –" he stopped again and gave me one of those looks like Mom had given me earlier. We watched the movie.

I couldn't concentrate, though. Instead, I laughed quietly to myself at Dad's excitement telling his story. Grandpa used to say that if you gave Dad a blank book, he could easily fill it with hundreds of stories. I thought about the apartment fire, imagining this little boy wanting to be a fireman. He was probably a lot younger than me, and here I am, none the wiser, just hoping to grow up.

Another commercial interrupted the movie, and I turned to Dad as soon as the bubbling brown drink appeared on the screen, "Dad, are you happy? Fighting fires and stuff? Was college a waste of time for you?"

He smiled like a father smiles at his daughter for getting an A or passing a test. "I used to, I used to feel guilty that I had spent all that time and money learning something I never fully put to use; but I don't feel that way now." He put his newspaper down and leaned toward me on his right elbow. "See, Mac, I just wanted to get out of college and marry your mother, start raising a family and have a good job, one that could support the life we wanted, and still give me time to be with my kids.

"I just really wanted to fight fires, but I thought her folks," his eyebrows raised toward Mom, "would want some businessman, someone respectable. And then I realized that it was my life and I could still make good money - it was saving peoples' lives that seemed important. I realized it's not if you're a doctor or a farmer or a judge or a fireman. That's not what's important because that's not really you. You're what's inside the uniform.

"A man is what he says, what he feels in his heart, not what he puts on in the morning or how much he brings home at the end of the week.

"Look at Uncle Frank," he paused dramatically, sighed, and continued, "what money's done to him. Money claimed him long ago. He's got too much self-importance now. At that point, you sort of cease being a man; you cease being anything at all. Because if you see the world as you being better than others, then others will see the world as them being better than you. That's not the world I want to be in."

Dad stopped and looked over at Mom who had turned her head from the television and was now listening to her husband. His eyes glistened, but he wasn't crying. He just gazed over at mom.

Then he looked back at me, "Mac, you know all your

mother and I want" *oh, God, here it comes* "is for you to be happy. Whatever that is to you. And we'll always love you. We just want you and your brothers to be happy, healthy, not have money worries, to just live happy lives.

"But, unfortunately, that means you'll need to plan for having money, jobs that make money, because America isn't a welfare state. You know, this country where the rich man lives across the street, around the corner, or up the stairs from the poor man; this country makes you work for a living, it makes you earn your keep. Like it or not, right or wrong, that's the way it is, the way it'll always be.

"You gotta realize that you can't climb trees the rest of your life or plan secret clubs with Paisley or go to India and hide away in the mountains; you have to face Life, and Life here in the US, in California, means working. In a hospital, an office, a burning building, a hole in the ground. That's Life.

"Just don't forget the other part, the part that's you, your heart, your kindness, your honesty. That's also Life, and that's the real part to pay attention to, not lose touch with."

Dad reached over and poured himself a cup of hot tea, adding a lemon squirt and several teaspoons of sugar. He tasted it. Just right. Not too sweet, not too sour.

I thought about what he said about climbing trees. I gulped. No, I couldn't gulp. Something caught in my throat. Like a piece of bark, a lump of sap. My tree was in me, part of me. A whisper passed through me. I stood up and walked away. Hurried. Through the kitchen doors. Out of the house.

I had to get there, up there. Why was my heart pounding? Unlatching the back door, turning the knob, feeling slow and clumsy, I ran through the back patio and out the side gate, across the front lawn. I felt the wet winter grass tickle my bare feet.

There it was. I gazed. I breathed in, out, slowly, calming myself.

There it was, the stump, the remains of my tree-climbing

days. Was Dad right? Was it time to grow up? Stop climbing trees? I walked over, sat on the round, hard, cool surface, looked up at the sky and wept.

It couldn't be true. That was just Dad talk. Didn't he know, this girl climbs trees; and if climbing trees stops by age 13, then I would turn back time to being 12. I would simply stay 12. For the rest of my life.

25

THE SENSE OF SCENTS

That mystery box hasn't moved from its spot in the front hall since Friday night. It mocks me, sitting there quietly teasing, *Haha, I know what's inside and you don't.*

Dad just tells me to leave it. When I bug Mom, I get, "Later, later. Not now." Okay, so there can't be anything living in there, or it'd be dead by now. Why don't they just open the box? Testing my patience, are they?

Maybe it's ...

Sunday, January 7, 1979, age 13, Grandma's old place

While Grandma settled in New York with Uncle Bert, Marc and I drove with Mom to Las Palimas to clean out the apartment and pack up some of Grandma's belongings.

Marc kept saying that Grandma should've just moved into a senior's home while she was here because she knew that as soon as Grandpa died she would move in with Bert.

Mom said nothing. Her silence signaled her anger at Marc's words. Then, after five minutes, "Marc, you need to think before you speak. You know Grandma wasn't thinking clearly. Who would be? She, we, everyone did the best they could."

We pulled into the parking garage, unloaded some cleaning supplies and headed into the apartment. The whole time, Mom didn't say a word to Marc. And Marc, he just apologized then went into the hall to mop. This brother had long ago earned the title of always coming off innocent while making everyone else feel things were their fault.

Entering the apartment, I felt as though no one had lived there in years. At the same time, it felt like a home my grandparents had lived in all their lives, just not recently. The only trace of life: sweet scents of Grandma's fruity perfume. No Grandpa smells, though, since he'd never lived there.

Too bad, I loved his smell, so warm and cuddly, like a bed you've just woken up in after a winter night's sleep. If I had really wanted to smell Grandpa now, I would have to walk to the hospital and enter that sterile room with machine guards and soldier hooks.

The smell wouldn't be Grandpa, though. It'd be rubbing alcohol and stale plastic hospital air. That wasn't how I wanted to remember his smell, but it seemed that whenever I'd now visit someone in a hospital, I'd think of him. I tried to conjure up the old house on Fourth Street and Grandpa's reading chair. How every time we'd stop by, he'd be sitting there reading a book, and by his side would lay a bowl of hard colorful sweets that he'd suck on endlessly as part of his reading routine.

I hated them. They tasted like, like nothing – if nothing had a taste. Mom said that was because Grandpa had developed diabetes and couldn't take sugar. Seemed ironic that in his old age, Life had robbed him of the sweetness of the world, literally.

It took us the whole day to clean out the apartment, packing all Grandma's clothes and knick-knacks. She told Mom to take all of Grandpa's clothes to our house for Dad and the boys or just give them away to one of the firemen's charities, like my dolls. She didn't want to have anything to do with them. She's also given us all his books. They're mostly about war, a few spy ones and the entire collection of Sherlock Holmes. I asked for the set. Perhaps I sensed the oncoming mystery.

You see, at the end of the day, something out of the ordinary happened. Marc and I were taking several bags of charity stuff to the car while Mom offered one final vacuum and dust. Mom always says a home can never be too clean.

After I'd squeezed my third and last bulging green garbage bag into the back seat, I took a short rest and looked around the deserted street. This was the inland part of Las Palimas. Not near the coastal homes that Paisley visited each summer. Mostly old people lived in this neighborhood, which consisted of paint-peeling orange and yellow apartment buildings – no houses, no children playing in yards, and no little dogs running about. Or so I thought.

A rustling noise caught my attention. A quick glance up and down the street led my eye to spy an invader. Near a small group of gray trashcans at the end of Grandma's driveway, a little scavenger lurked, a small brown dog. Probably a stray. So thin, I figured it hadn't eaten in days. I whistled to it. After looking out from behind the tipped over can, it cautiously approached, stopping just a few feet before me.

"Hello little puppy. Are you hungry fella?" I asked. It glanced up, staring intently at me through big dark eyes. "How about some crackers? Would you like that? Wait here then." I pointed my finger toward the ground. "Don't run away, I'll be right back. Stay," I commanded, holding my right hand out like a traffic cop then turned, ran back to the apartment, and grabbed a box of crackers off the kitchen counter.

I returned, surprised, yet pleased. The little dog appeared not to have budged. He sat on the sidewalk wagging his tail as I approached. Maybe he just had nowhere to be.

"Here you go, boy," I took a few crackers out of the red box. "Come on, boy, here you go. It's all right, I won't hurt you." But it just stared at me. So I tossed a few down on the ground. It backed away, frightened, as if I had thrown the crackers *at* him. Then slowly, it moved toward them, gobbling each one down within seconds. I tried to pat his head. Wrong move. He snapped at me. I think he even growled.

It didn't break the skin or anything, just kind of scared me. I dropped the box of crackers and ran crying into the apartment for Marc. "What's wrong?"

"That dog bit me," I said with tears dripping down my cheeks.

"What dog? Here let me see you. Oh, it's nothing, Mac. Did it scare ya?"

"Yes," my crying turned to sobbing and I grabbed hold of my comfort brother.

He patted my back, "It's okay. Come on, where's he at? Take me to him."

"Outside, but don't hurt it, Marc. It didn't know. I just thought it looked hungry, and ... I don't know. I just wanted to help it."

Marc walked down the driveway and started yelling at the dog that had its nose deep inside the cracker box.

"Get outta here!" he yelled as he ran toward the dog. "Go on, get! Shoo!"

"Don't hit it, Marc. Look, it's going. See."

"Yeah, okay," Marc threw down a small stone intended for the poor dog. "You're not bleedin' are ya? Let me see." I gave him my hand. "No, you're all right. It'll just be sore, but as long as it didn't bite into the skin, you'll be okay. You know, you could've gotten rabies, Mac. Don't do that next time. Get me. Dogs are unpredictable."

"Yeah, tell me about it," I proclaimed. Tears gone, I was in recovery now. "You know, it looked hungry, and it wagged its tail when I first moved toward it. But then, I don't know, after I fed it, it just turned mean."

Marc picked up the empty cracker box and tossed it into the big dumpster. We both walked back inside to finish packing. I turned back to find the dog. The streets lay as empty as when I'd first come outside. No kids, no dogs. The only evidence – a few cracker crumbs on the sidewalk.

I showed Mom my hand. She just said I shouldn't go near dogs and cats and that, anyway, I should've been loading the car. Yeah, I know feeding stray dogs is foolish, but sometimes you just need to take a chance because it feels more right than foolish. Mom doesn't get that.

During the long ride home, I couldn't help considering what that brown dog had to do with people; how we think someone's nice, but the first chance they get, they hurt you. Boys are like that.

Joe Basketball, too. He smiles at me whenever I cheer him at games, but in the halls, I don't exist. After all, what am I in the halls? On the court, I'm a fan, not Eliza. He doesn't see me, he just sees fans. Like the dog just saw I had food then when I didn't have food, it didn't want anything to do with me. It didn't smell me or try to find out who I was.

The ride home seemed to take forever, but we finally reached the last traffic light before turning up the windy road and down our little street. That particular stoplight always stays red for ages. As we sat there, I glanced out my left-side window. Although it was January, the day hadn't seen much rain. The roads looked dry.

Out of the blue, an unseasonably crisp brown leaf gently fell to the roadway. I watched it lay softly down on the hard black surface as cars whizzed past from around the corner. Every time a car drove by, the leaf seemed to jump out of the way. I hoped nothing crushed it as it innocently lay there like a small child who didn't know any better.

Then as I feared, a large truck came barreling around the corner. Just as its huge rubber tire rolled swiftly up behind the leaf, some mystical force stepped in and the truck's approach pushed the leaf to safety. Had the leaf sensed oncoming danger and moved itself away? Without cue, it lay gently back on the ground ready to perform its next magical acrobatic feat. Instantly, I knew. I smiled. Grandpa.

As the light turned green and we moved on, Benjie's four-year-old face flashed in my mind. I couldn't help wishing he had had that same sense, that same knowing to move out of the way of Michael Hayes' car. I wondered why the Goddess hadn't warned Benjie as She had that leaf, urged him to just jump back onto the curb.

Most people have this sense; they just don't listen to it. I suppose it's like what Grandpa said about believing in myself and listening for that voice. Listening to my voice and not just Paisley's.

I think Pais just has more sense about things than I do. Like, she wouldn't have petted that dog. She would've been more like that leaf and moved out of the way before she'd gotten bit. But that's Paisley, always knowing what to do.

I do have a sense of knowing, too, Grandpa. Surely, it has to be inside me somewhere.

26

DOUBLE DRAMA

As far as elementary school went, most of my fond memories remained on the playground where I could talk to Paisley and where Peggy Marsh taught me the f word.

After a few years of junior high, I've noticed the classroom has some lessons to offer, too.

I know that someday soon I will understand exactly what to do with my life; and that someday soon that unfamiliar little voice will be as familiar to me as my own face.

Of course, right now, today, this teen certainly has no answers to what Life's all about. I mean, how does a girl plan her future while she's still trying to figure out how to live the present?

More importantly, how can I grow up when some days I feel like I'm growing down? Today was one of those days.

Double drama.

Monday, January 8, 1979, 13 going on three?, Park View Junior High

Just a few weeks ago, I finished what I think is my favorite book, *The Outsiders*. Of course, the main character's a boy, but it's about friendship, and that's what spoke to me. I've been thinking about my friendship with one Paisley Emma Park. I've been thinking how I let jealousy get in the way of things, of things like love and loyalty. Jealousy is exactly what reared its ugly head for me today in English.

Paisley. I love her like a sister, but I envy her brains and how she sticks to her beliefs. I want to be proud of her and me, not jealous. Sometimes, I feel so proud of myself, so full of myself, when I'm praised for something and Paisley's not.

Jealousy is bad enough, but pride that leads to arrogance is more sinful yet. I'm not arrogant, I don't think. I try to be me, true to myself; even if it means I need to show my jealousies or insecurities. It goes back to trusting yourself, listening to what that little voice thinks.

Unfortunately for me, I don't always listen to that voice.

The mini drama, English class, third period

Every month, Ms. Eben asks us to write a poem on a particular theme. It's usually connected to what we're studying. In September, it was about making new friends. Last month, December, war. This month's theme: Simple Life. It had to do with people returning to a simple life after the Revolutionary War, which is what we studied in history.

Today, Ms. Eben announced the month's winner. Today, I sat as usual expecting to hear Paisley or Shelley's names called. Today was not what I expected.

"Here's a lovely poem this month." Ms. Eben stood before us with a stack of papers. "I'd like to read it out to you. Listen to the voice. Listen to the rhythm."

I fidgeted in my seat, twirling my pencil between my fingers like a gymnast at the Olympics. Of course, it'd be Paisley's poem. Ms. Eben loved Paisley's work. I could feel the stinging bites of jealousy crawl up my spine. In fact, I'd read her poem. It was incredible.

Ms. Eben began.

> *Gentle wind across the plain;*
> *swirling sand that ends my pain.*
> *Cascading clouds parade the sky;*
> *turkey vulture flying high.*
> *I witness all in glory time;*
> *I witness life in sweet sublime.*
> *Hearts that fill with desert sand;*
> *cracking skin across my hand.*
> *Gentle winds don't fill my heart;*
> *sky-high clouds tear me apart.*
> *I witness all in glory time.*
> *I witness life in sweet sublime.*

My heart pounded as soon as I heard the words. Those were my words, my poem. Not Paisley's. I barely heard Ms. Eben say "Maclyn", "winner", "January".

Then it rose up. Not jealous pins, but prideful, boastful, superior air circulated in my head. I was dizzy. I was happy. I was the winner, not Paisley. And within an instant, I wanted to sink as deep down in the ground as possible, to crawl right under my desk but first to run over to Pais and apologize for thoughts she never heard me utter.

Instead, I did nothing.

It was Paisley whose smile stretched broader than any, who reached over and gave my arm a squeeze, who whispered, "way to go, Eliza. So cool!"

I gulped, took in a deep sigh, and smiled. "Yeah, pretty cool."

The mega drama, Paisley's turn, lunchtime, the yard

By lunch, my pride had deflated, my guilt had collected and solidified somewhere in my left toe, and Paisley Park sat before me ranting on about her new hot topic: careers.

Paisley never gives up when she knows she's right about something. That's her strength and flaw. Double-edged sword, as Kenny might say. She'll put up a fight to the very end. Today was no different. Randy Miles and her got into a lulu. He always calls Pais a know-it-all (which she is and knows but doesn't like being reminded) and tells her she's too pushy for a girl.

One time, in sixth grade, I thought they were going to have a fistfight over it. Luckily, they didn't. Luckily, for Randy, they didn't because John F has taught Pais karate knowing his little sister has a big mouth in need of protection.

Today's argument nearly ended in a brawl, too. Pais made a valiant attempt to put Randy in his place; however, he didn't hang around long enough for her to do that.

The lunch bell rang, putting a close to Mr. Finley's fourth period science class and our guest speaker's lecture. A doctor, a *woman* doctor, had spent 40 minutes discussing her job in the hospital. Her pitch focused on girls being anything they want these days, just like the boys. She named women in history like Elizabeth Blackwell who'd changed the world.

Out on the picnic tables at lunch, Amy, Pais, Randy, Roger Thomas and I began by discussing the usual topics (who's going with who, what someone got on a test, stuff like that), until Randy decided to say something stupid.

"That lady doctor sure was boring. What a goof." His thoughtless words hung in the air only briefly, awaiting a swat from Paisley. "My doctor's a man. I wouldn't trust a woman looking at me. No way! No woman is gonna look at me naked, not even my mom."

Then it happened. Paisley put down her sandwich. We each paused our meals. She stood, hands on her narrow hips, ponytail flying in the breeze, and a narrow gaze aimed straight for Randy Miles, "And what do you think you know, Randy? What makes you the expert on what jobs women should have?"

Clearly caught off-guard, Randy stuttered, "Whhwhhat? Whaddya mean? I was just sayin-"

"You were just blah-blah-blahing, Randy, that's what you were doing. Not thinking. Just talking. Talking nonsense." She glared at his round face, framed by a growing band of red, topped off with his new crew cut. "You, of all people, have no right saying that Dr. May doesn't know anything and shouldn't even be a doctor. She sounds like a great doctor to me. Just like Dr. McCloud, and he doesn't even work in the hospital. He only looks up little kids' noses. What makes him any better than Dr. May?"

Randy suddenly located his nerve. "Just because she's a doctor in a hospital doesn't mean she's any smarter than Doc McCloud. Anyways, men are always smarter," oh, God, he didn't just say that, did he? "My daddy says it's just in men to be smarter because they have to take care of the women and children. It's genetic. Why do you think there haven't been many women doctors anyway? Face it, men are naturally smarter."

Paisley's calmness frightened me. Amy stepped back one. "Oh," replied Paisley with an odd little smile. "I see. So, well, then, why are there women doctors now?"

Randy stared at Pais, and for a second there, I thought he was going to take a swing at her, but he just stared. Then he looked at Roger who was trying to hold back a laugh.

Randy tried some diversionary tactics. "What are you smiling at, Roger? Huh? This ain't funny. This here's serious, so you better just stop smiling, or I'll have to wallop you, too." Roger stopped smiling. After all, he and Randy have been close friends since third grade.

"What do you mean 'wallop you, too'? No way you'd get anywhere near me, Randy. Anyway, all of this is funny. So, answer my question. Why are there women doctors now?" Paisley stared.

"You're too pushy, Paisley. You are way too pushy for a girl. You've been pushy since I met you in the third grade. You oughta be more like Amy. She's quiet. Mac ain't pushy neither. Why don't you be more like them?"

"I am not pushy. I have asked you a question and you are being a big chicken not answering it, that's what's going on here."

"You got too much of that women's lib stuff in you. That's your problem. You're never gonna get married because you are just too darn pushy. That's probably how that lady got to be a doctor. She just pushed people so much they got tired of her and said, 'here, be a doctor, lady, just leave us alone!' "

Roger laughed. "Hey, I warned you, Roger. Don't laugh at me." Though Roger liked hanging out with Randy, he was no fan of his anger. Roger swallowed nervously.

"You don't have to listen to him, Roger. You do whatever you want," Paisley assured him in her mother's voice then turned back to Randy and continued. "Now you, Randy. What was that you were saying about women's lib?"

"You got too much of that stuff in you. My daddy says women think too much and are beginning to think they are like men. My mamma never worked. Daddy wouldn't allow it. She don't want to work neither. Says the woman's place is in the home, raising the kids, taking care of the house. She knows she doesn't belong in a hospital unless she's sick or gonna have a baby."

How could Paisley take this? I was ready to wallop him myself, but I was too busy worrying about Roger and feeling sorry for Randy's mom. "That makes no sense. You've said nothing that makes any sense at all. All I've heard you say is probably what your Dad's said to you. Don't you think for yourself?" Paisley had inched closer to Randy, her hands still resting on her hips. Paisley invaded his space. Randy clearly took this body language as a threat.

"Just get it. Women belong at home!" Randy yelled, small beads of spit shot out of his mouth. "How about your mom. Does she work?"

"She volunteers at the Santa Nina Arts Council."

"She get paid?"

"Volunteers, dummy, don't get paid."

"Then it ain't no job."

"It is. She is a volunteer. Who says a job means getting paid. That's such a man's way of seeing things."

"Look, it ain't no flippin' job if you don't get paid!"

"I'm done here with you, Randy. You're just too thick. My mom volunteers for an organization that doesn't have the money to pay for help because all of the government's money goes to soldiers – boys not much older than you – fighting stupid wars all over the world. Soldiers who get shot and hurt and need to go to hospitals to get well and don't care if the doctor's a man or a woman, just as long as they get better.

"There's nothing wrong with a woman staying home with her children if that's what she wants to do. But if she wants to work, if she wants to go fight a stupid war, then a woman should be able to do that. Besides, my dad and brother help out around the house just like a family should. John F cooks and so does my dad. And we are all very proud of my mom for everything she does. If your mom doesn't choose to work, then that's fine. For her. It doesn't have to be the same for every woman."

"My mom works," piped in Amy, probably just as surprised at her input as the rest of us.

"I wasn't asking you!" Randy shot out. When he turned from her, Amy stuck out her tongue. Roger swallowed a chuckle. "You all just butt out! This is between me and Paisley."

"Randy, Amy was just tryin-" I began, feeling the call to rescue the needy.

"Hey, I said Butt Out!" He turned toward Paisley, "You just don't know what you're talking about. Neither do any of you. I've had enough." Suddenly, it dawned on me. Randy didn't just want to be right. He wanted Paisley to see he was right. He liked her.

The lunch bell rang. We started to gather up our books for fifth period.

Paisley didn't say a thing. No one did. Not being able to

stand the silence, I yelled after Randy, "Me, Paisley and Amy are all going to be important one day, Randy, and you'll be sorry! I'm telling you, you'll see!" Roger laughed then turned and ran to catch up with his friend.

Pais just started walking toward the main building. Amy and I followed.

I could tell that conversation ended on the yard. Anyway, I know my suspicions are right. Randy's Paisley's lab partner in science. He picked her. I don't think he has a chance, though. Randy Miles is not Paisley Park's type. If you want to get on her good side, you gotta let her be right – at least most of the time.

Now that Paisley's decided to be a vet, she will be a real doctor one day; and boy will Randy be sorry. Of course, she won't work in a hospital, but she'll be a doctor. And a doctor's a doctor, whether your patients are animals or people.

Besides, it's like Dad said, it's not the uniform that matters but the person inside. If Randy ends up being a doctor and Pais a housewife, I'll still have more respect for Paisley than for him, even if he does work in a hospital. Pais is a good person inside.

Randy could learn a lot from her.

27

FOUR WHITE MICE

Okay, so no, if you are wondering. The answer is: not yet. The box sits unopened. I am about ready to get a scissor or razor and start slicing some secret opening. I figure if I do it in such a way, in the back, and take a peak, no one will know. They'll think it got damaged in the airplane.

I haven't yet, but I might. I've done some sneaky things in my time. In fact, last night might be the topper.

Ever since Pais and I stopped eating animals that summer before sixth grade and formed our secret organization, we've performed little deeds here and there to stop other people from hurting animals. Paisley even got a letter published in the newspaper asking people not to eat meat. Kenny said they only published it because she was 11 years old and they probably thought it was 'cute'. I don't think so. It was a good letter written intelligently about serious matters. Eric said Kenny didn't know what he was talking about and not to listen to him, that Paisley's letter was a good idea.

This past summer, we sent a petition around the neighborhood asking for the animal shelter to keep stray dogs and cats for ten days before they put them to sleep. Everyone signed it, and the shelter extended the time from three days to ten. I tried to get Dad to adopt one or two dogs, but he wasn't interested. I don't think he wanted to deal with more dogs running away and getting hit. Rowan is enough.

Dad has a big heart. After all, he spends every working day trying to save people's lives. Yet when it comes to a cute furry dog or even a mean stray that likes crackers, he just doesn't have the time to care. Sure, maybe it's money. I get that. I know my brothers would chip in. I just like having lots of animals around. Guess that's what comes from growing up with four brothers. The chaos, noise and mess just feel homey.

I think I might even save a dog from a burning building before I'd rescue a person - especially if that person were anything like Mr. Finley. He's the pits, a murderer, a mad scientist who kills pigs, frogs and mice.

Tuesday, January 9, 1979, 13 again

Actually, Pais calls anyone who eats animals a murderer. Everyday I have to remind myself why I don't eat animals. Sometimes I crave a hamburger - just salivate for that fleshy, juicy beef. I have to intervene quickly (especially if Dad's barbequing). I just take out my animal welfare magazines and look at pictures of farms and slaughterhouses. That usually does the trick.

So we use our organization to meet and plan events. Doing little deeds now will lead up to the final day when we really let the world know that we mean business. Of course, that final day's a secret. Since we can't really do anything big at the moment, we have to do what we can. (We absolutely have no idea what the "big" thing will be, but it gives us something to look forward to.)

Up until last night, our feats have included: recruiting more girls and convincing them of the vegetarian life;

sending around petitions to stop or change laws and rules unfair to animals; and writing letters to newspapers about cruelty to animals.

So about last night .... It wasn't a difficult task – in fact, it possessed elements of excitement – I really thought we were going to get caught. For sure people suspect us. Students, that is. Teachers haven't a clue. Most of them never really know their students as individuals. They just see the outer package. If you just sit in class and say nothing (which is what most of them hope you'll do), you can pass through school unnoticed and undisturbed. Those who want to be noticed find ways.

Of course, Paisley's quite outspoken, so you'd think some teacher might wise up to her. Perhaps they just don't care. Paisley says she'll tell Mr. Finley the day after he turns in our last semester grades. I'd prefer she stays quiet. I don't need the attention.

In honor of this New Year, 1979, we decided to test out our mice-freeing scheme. Amy thought we should've done it on Parents' Night in May, but we couldn't wait. Anyway, Pais said, too many possible witnesses. It might've been good publicity, but we didn't want to risk any chance of spoiling our mission. So we decided on a quiet Tuesday evening after everyone had left the school grounds. Only we hadn't anticipated anyone who might be lingering about later, and we came near a very close call. Close but not close enough.

I left my house at seven, telling my unsuspecting parents that Paisley was helping me with an essay. We pedaled our bikes the six blocks to school, picking up Amy and Heather on the way. Wearing the darkest clothes we could find, we enjoyed our little Charlie's Angels adventure.

We arrived at school by 7:15 as planned and rolled our bikes in through the back gates, across the dirt track. A few ground lights supplied us with enough visibility to lock our getaway rides and hop inside the science building through an open window.

Paisley had cleverly left her sweater in class that morning so she could return at the end of the day to collect it just as Mr. Finley would be locking the door. She ran in and opened a ground window while he waited outside, grabbed her sweater and ever so kindly thanked him.

Then last night Pais climbed in through the window and let the three of us in via the main door. The dark classroom allowed us to remain in the shadows. Opening the blinds offered enough moonlight to fill the room and light our way. The cages reflected small streams of light making them easy to spot. Only two cages sat on the back table, each containing two white mice.

Mr. Finley had separated them, not by sex – they were all females – but merely by random for an experiment the class was to conduct next week. He'd said the test consisted of feeding the mice in the left cage a regular diet of lettuce, grains and other veggies, and feeding the right caged mice sugar, cookies and other junk food. After a week, we would see what a poor diet could do to the mice, and thus to us. Well, we then realized this meant the right caged mice might die or at the least get real sick. You see, we had no choice - we had to free them.

We didn't want to take too long or our folks might start phoning each other's houses when we had all said we would be at the other person's house. If my mom phoned the Parks, they'd say they thought Paisley was at my house, and oh boy would we be in a heap of trouble. If we could get out by quarter to eight, we could be home by nine and no one would be the wiser. The plan almost worked perfectly. Almost.

"Hurry up, now, Amy. Get the shoeboxes," Paisley commanded. Mr. Finley always kept several cardboard boxes in his back cupboard. We each had a task. I was to line the boxes with shredded newspaper that I had borrowed from Dad's evening edition. Heather was to unlock the cages and help Pais put the mice in the boxes.

"Come on, you guys. We need three boxes. We don't have a lot of time. Hurry. That looks good. Okay."

"How many mice are you taking, Heather?"

"Eliza, be quiet. No talking," Pais snapped at me then turned to Heather and whispered, "Now, how many mice do you want, Heather?"

"I'll just take one of them for my little brother, and Amy wants one, too. What're you going to do with the other two?"

"No problem. I'll take them home tonight, then to-" Pais interrupted herself. "Come on, we haven't got much time left. Make sure there are plenty of air holes in the lids. Heather, do you have the lettuce?"

"Yeah, it's in my pocket. We had tacos tonight, so-"

"Okay, shh, come on," Pais was in rare form, clearly enjoying her little power trip. "Okay, Amy, make sure all three boxes have plenty of lettuce. Hurry."

I poked holes as fast as I could – evidently not fast enough for Paisley who glared at me from behind the cages. After I'd finished the third box, I handed it to Heather. "That one's for the two. It has the most lettuce," I told her. She unlocked the cage and held the box ready for the mice.

Just as Pais started to open the tiny gate, we heard someone fiddling about at the door. It sounded like the clinking of a key ring. A beam of light flashed across the ceiling and wall.

"Oh, no, someone's here. Oh, God, what're we gonna do?" I whispered in a panic.

"Calm down. There - we can hide in Mr. Finley's dark room. Come on now. Someone grab those boxes."

Just as we all scurried into the tiny closet-like room, the door opened. We could only hold our breath and hope it wasn't old Mr. Baldy.

"My, my these kids're gettin' messier and messier every day. My, my," a heavy voice spoke. "Hmm, these teachers ain't much help either, heh, heh." We could hear a broom's bristles brush across the floor.

"It's only Richard, the janitor," Paisley assured us.

"He has a lovely singing voice," Heather whispered.

"Yeah, well, he had better hurry it up or we're gonna have a lot of explaining to do to a lotta adults."

"He'll be out quick enough," I comforted Paisley and the rest. "Listen, he's near the mice. Did you lock the cage back up?"

"Oh, no!" Heather exclaimed.

"Shh! We don't want to alarm him."

"Now, what's this? Hello there little fellas. I never seen you before. Was you in here last night? Well, ain't you all cute. Heh, heh, heh." He continued sweeping and humming. "Ain't nobody here, but us chickens," sweep, sweep, "ain't nobody here at all...."

"Hurry up, Richard," Pais whispered softly. Then we heard him switch off the light and close the door.

Slowly, Amy opened the dark room's door and peeked out. "All clear."

We hurried out and resumed our mission. Pais carefully placed the first two mice in a box.

"What're you going to do with those ones?" Heather asked.

"I'll keep them in my room tonight then tomorrow I'll take them to the lake."

"Won't the squirrels or cats up there get them?" asked Amy. "The field on the other side of your street would probably be safer, don't you think?"

"Yeah, probably so. I'll take them there instead." Then Paisley placed the mouse from the right cage in the shoebox. "Here Amy, you hold that, put a rubber band around it. I'll carry it home."

"Now, where is the second box ... thanks ... this first one'll be for you, Amy." She gently placed a tiny white one from the left cage into the box and handed it to her.

"This is for you, Heather. All right?"

"Yeah, she's cute. Danny'll love him. That Mr. Finley is so cruel."

"Okay, that's it. Mission accomplished. Now, Eliza, check

the door. See if anyone's outside. Richard, anyone."

"No one. Coast is clear."

Everyone carried a box except me. Then we mounted our bikes and rode off home. The mission had been successful, and I arrived home by 8:30 without a word from either parent.

This morning, before school, I accompanied Paisley to the open field at the end of our street. We let the two little mice go after having fed them a big meal of raw rice and lettuce. I asked Pais about the snakes and coyotes in the field.

She just said, "Better to leave these animals' lives up to nature than to Mr. Finley's redundant experiments. Doesn't he think we know soda and junk food aren't good for us? We don't need to kill mice to get it."

Mr. Finley announced the mice's disappearance in class and asked for any information. He said he had questioned Richard, but that he'd seen the mice in their cages when he was cleaning.

"I never thought we might get Richard into trouble," Paisley admitted after class. "We had better do something." After school, we borrowed Paisley's mom's typewriter and crafted a note. We'll slip it under Baldy's door tomorrow before school.

WE HAVE FREED THE MICE FROM YOUR CRUEL EXPERIMENT. RICHARD IS INNOCENT. DO NOT PURCHASE ANY MORE MICE OR OTHER ANIMALS OR WE WILL RETURN.
   SIGNED,
FOUR NICE MICE PEOPLE

The episode will probably die down after a few weeks.

I wonder if old Mr. Finley will replace the mice or conduct any other experiments on living animals. I don't know if we really convinced him that what he was doing was wrong. I hope so.

If he does get more mice, it's Charlie's Angels one more time. I think Grandpa would be proud of me.

28

ONE BROTHER SHINES A LIGHT

That's it. Mom says we can't open the box for another week. She said she's not ready. I'm ready. Maybe if it didn't sit there staring at me, mocking me on a daily basis. How about the closet, or garage? No, she said, it needs to be where it is.

Fine.

To be honest, though, that box is starting to really give me the creeps. It doesn't bother me in the day so much, but as soon as it's time for bed, I worry. Not just about the box, about everything. I get this far away feeling in my head and then I just think about dying. It seems death, darkness, sleep, they all go together. Since it's winter, there's not much sun and the days are so gray and gloomy.

When I get home from school and go upstairs to do my homework, I find myself more than not daydreaming, staring in far-away thought out my bedroom window, up towards that place in the sky where you can't really see any further but just keep looking anyway.

There seems to be something that draws me out there. Sometimes I feel it's a waste of time to daydream, but then I feel that maybe writing a history essay is even more meaningless. I wish I could just grow up and know things. It's this not knowing thing that's hard. Not knowing what I'm supposed to do, or be, or just what it's all about.

Thursday, January 11, 1979, still 13

Ever since Grandpa died, I've been obsessed with death. For the first few weeks, I couldn't go to sleep at night without thinking that maybe I wouldn't wake up in the morning; maybe I'd just die in my sleep, like Grandpa. I have such terrible nightmares, too. Last night, I dreamt I was a duck, a white fluffy one with a bright orange bill. I think the mice incident has infected my conscience.

Waddling around with all these other ducks, I collected hard-boiled eggs from the frying pans. Some of the eggs were already cracked, and powdery yellow yolks spilled out. There was this man, a farmer or something who looked so much like Mr. Finley. He started inspecting us to see which ones would be killed and which ones would stay with him.

I kept screaming in the dream that it didn't matter if we weren't chosen by Farmer Finley this time 'round because eventually we were all going to be slaughtered.

I must have been screaming out loud because I awoke to Marc and Kevin. Apparently my screams interrupted their music. Hearing my shrieks, they ran into my room to see what was happening. When I looked at the clock, I was amazed to see it read 12:15. I remembered being awake at five-to.

"Mac, ya okay? What happened? Ya okay?" Marc asked, shaking me awake. "Kev, turn on the light."

I blinked my eyes open, seeing for the first time my brothers' frightened faces. Then I remembered my dream, and I reached up to hug Marc. He patted my back gently.

"Ah, it's okay. Bad dream? Come on now, calm down and tell us what happened."

"Oh it was the weirdest dream I've ever had," I shivered. "I was a duck. I dreamt I was a duck."

"A duck." Kevin repeated. Did he laugh, too?

"Yeah. A big white one. With an orange beak. Oh, it was so scary because the farmer, who looked a lot like Mr. Finley, was going to kill us and there were all these eggs and a frying pan, and we were all running, and –"

"Slow down, Mac. C'mon. That doesn't sound too scary."

"Maybe it was to her, Marc, how would you know?" Kevin defended me then turned and asked, "Was the farmer shooting at you with a gun?"

"Ah, c'mon, Kev, farmers don't kill animals with guns. They just hit 'em over the head or break their necks or something like that."

"Oh, that's nice. I'm sure Mac likes hearing that," Kevin turned to me, forgetting perhaps that I didn't care about what they thought, I just wanted to share what had happened.

"There wasn't a gun. I don't think, oh, I don't remember."

"Come on, Mac, why don't' you just lie down and go back to sleep. Relax."

"Maybe she's still upset. Do you want a glass of water?" Kevin offered.

"No, I'm okay, thanks, though. I guess I should try to go back to sleep. It's just that, it all seemed so real. You know? I never dreamt I was duck before or anything like that. I wonder if it's a message or something. Do you think it means something?"

"Naw, it don't mean nothing. It's a dream, that's all."

"You don't know that. It could mean something," Kevin turned to me. "Maybe tomorrow we can go to the library and look it up in one of those dream books. I've seen a bunch of them there. They're kinda cool. Want to?"

"Yeah, that'd be good," I said, feeling better already. I've always thought of Kevin as my invisible brother. He's never really around, and when he is, he's in his room. He's always been the quiet thinker of the family (me being the loud thinker; and Eric just being a plain old thinker). Lately, he's been hanging out with John F because they both go to Santa Nina Community College. John F gives Kevin rides. I've been wondering lately about them, but it's not really my business. I love them both, and so, if John F isn't interested in me, at least I get to see him when he comes to get Kevin.

Suddenly, I remembered why I was having nightmares. "Do you guys still think about Grandpa?"

"What?" Marc asked clearly caught off guard.

"I do," Kevin interjected. "I think about him but not a lot." He paused. "Is that why you've been having these bad dreams lately? Do you miss him?"

"Yeah. I miss him, and ... and," I heaved a heavy sigh, "and I'm afraid of dying, too. It's all I think about these days."

"Well, we're all going to die some day, Mac. But you're just 13, so you've got a long ways before you kick the bucket," spoke my dear brother Marc.

"Nice," Kevin teased. "We don't really know when we're gonna die, though. Take little Benjie. He was only four. It happens whenever. Mac, you don't need to worry about any of this now. Just be careful crossing streets and talking to strangers, and you'll be fine. We're all gonna live long lives. Don't worry yourself about death at 13. Don't smoke, don't be stupid, you'll be fine."

"Yeah, Kev's actually right – for once," Marc softly jabbed Kevin in the arm. "You're gonna live a long time. All of us will. Well, Grandpa was almost 80. That's what happens when you get old."

"But don't you guys ever think about dying? About what happens to us? Where do you think we go? Grandpa said he'd always be nearby. And sometimes I really feel him, but it's just so weird."

Marc and Kevin looked at each other. No one jumped in to answer me or say anything at all. Then finally, after what seemed like minutes but surely was just seconds, Marc stood up.

"Good girls go to Heaven."

"What?" Kevin and I queried in synchronicity.

"Good girls go to Heaven," he repeated seriously.

"That's your answer?" Kevin asked incredulously. "Where

did you get that?"

"Where's Heaven, anyway?" I asked.

"In the sky," Marc pointed out my window, "beyond the clouds, where you can't see any more, where you look up and wonder, what's up there? It's Heaven."

Kevin and I sat stunned by Marc's sudden spiritual understanding, his confidence in the subject, his ease, spoken as if he'd thought it out clearly long before this night. My comfort brother shed a moment of light on my dark world.

"How do you know that?" I needed more than just some poetic answer. I needed a guarantee.

"I don't know, really. That's just what I think. It just came to me one day when I was outside playing ball with Dad. He hit this really high fly ball, and when I looked up to catch it, the sun blinded me. So I just closed my eyes a minute and stuck out my glove. I felt the ball land. I couldn't believe it. Dad couldn't either. Then I looked up at the sky and felt like someone was up there watching me. It's just a feeling, that's all."

So, my girl-crazy brother has these feelings, too. He listens to his intuition and doesn't even know it.

"What do you think, Kev?" asked Marc, feeling quite the little philosopher at this moment.

"Um, I don't know. I guess if we're good, we go to Heaven, but I'm just not sure what 'good' means. If you trip a kid in fifth grade because he calls you a name, does that make you bad? Or do you need to do something really awful to be considered bad, like kill someone? I mean, what's good, what's bad?" *How about freeing a science teacher's collection of mice?* "I guess if I really think about it, when we die, we don't go to this 'Heaven' place or anywhere else. We just hang out around earth and all the humans we love, whether we were good or bad. Once you're dead, that stuff doesn't matter. It matters now, while you're alive."

"That makes sense to me," I told Kevin. "I think it's important what we do now, here. Whether you believe in

Heaven or anything else, what really matters is now."

"Yeah," Kevin pulled a string from his PJs, twirled it around his finger till the end turned red then white then he pulled it off and twisted it into a little ball.

"You know, I was alone in Grandpa's room just before he died. He told me lots of things. He said that I should learn to believe in myself and trust my instincts."

"That's good, but that's not to say you don't do the other things in life."

"What other things?"

"You know, being good, going to school, stuff like that."

"Well, yeah, I guess so, but I think he meant it's how you do those other things, how you think about them and stuff."

"Oh." Marc and Kevin stared at me as if *I* had the answers.

"Well, I'm tired and I gotta get up for practice, so let's go to sleep. Okay, Mac? Do you think you can go back to sleep now?"

"Yeah, I feel better. Thanks you guys," I hugged them both, giving each an extra squeeze but not feeling like I had to hang on. I could let go.

"Well, g'night, Mac, sweet dreams. We're just next door, if you need us."

"Thanks, Marc. Thanks, Kevin. See you in the morning."

"G'night, Mac," Kevin turned off the light and shut the door halfway. "I'll leave this open a bit in case you have another dream. G'night."

I don't think I'll dream about being a duck anymore, but I might have more nightmares. I just can't stop thinking about dying, though.

I wonder if I'll be able to fall asleep every night. Will I wake up worrying about dying? When I dream, will I meet Grandpa? Do trees dream? So much to know. So much wonder in this world.

I suppose if I can just be patient long enough, the answers will arrive.

29

ONE FRIEND SHARES SOME WISDOM

Paisley's been my best friend for about nine years now, nearly all my life. She's become such an important part of me, I sometimes scare myself thinking that one day she might just up and leave. Not move. Die.

If she died, a big part of me would go with her. Paisley's like a freckle. I mean, have you ever looked in the mirror and seen a freckle on your face that you hadn't noticed before? You can't remember if it had always been there or if it had just appeared overnight. That's how I feel with Pais sometimes.

Occasionally, I look in the mirror and see the freckle – and Paisley – for the very first time. Not that I've forgotten her; but she's become such a permanent part of me, I can – only for a moment – forget there had ever been a first meeting. So when I look into the mirror, now and again, it's like something new all over.

She's listened to all my fears about Grandpa, but I don't think she really gets it. Pais has never had someone close to her die; I don't think someone can really know exactly how it feels until they lose a friend or relative.

Would Paisley even cry at her own mother's funeral?

She's so serious and tries to make sense out of

everything. It might save her from a lot of hurt now, but it might also build up inside her until one day she just explodes.

Later Thursday night, January 11, 1979, still 13

After last night's duck and frying pan adventure, I remained hesitant to close my eyes. *Tossing. Turning. Tossing. Turning.* Before I knew it, it was midnight. Worrying about getting enough sleep had literally kept me from falling asleep. I wasn't even tired. Unfortunately, no one else in the house seemed to share my problem. I heard only silence. And that didn't help.

So I got up, slipped on my Calvin Klein's, boots, and heavy coat and let myself quietly out my window. As my maple no longer supplied me with a natural escape ladder, I had learned to skillfully climb down our ivy-covered trellis.

Darting across our dew-drenched lawn to Paisley's, I unlatched the Park's gate and let myself in their backyard. I climbed up her pine tree – much more difficult than my maple. Prickly needles covered its branches.

I tapped on her window. "Psst. Pais. It's me. Eliza. Open up."

A sleepy Paisley peeked through her blue and white-striped curtains then recognizing me, unlatched and opened her window. "What is it? What in the world are you doing, Eliza? It's after midnight. We have a big test in the morning, remember?"

"Yeah, but, I, um, just let me in. It's freezing out here!" Frost hugged the tree as clear skies showed no signs of rain.

"Come on then." Paisley helped me in. "Are you having trouble sleeping again? Nightmares?"

"Yeah. I've been lying in bed since ten and – achoo! – and I can't – achoo! –"

"Bless you. Here, take your coat off and wear my robe. It'll be warmer. Stay quiet. I'll go downstairs and make us some hot cocoa."

"Yeah, that sounds good – achoo!"

"Shh!" Paisley hurried down to the kitchen, momentarily leaving me to my sneezing and gloomy thoughts. I put on her soft warm velour robe and sat sniffling by the window. A myriad of stars and one bright moon nearly full but for a missing fingernail sliver scattered across the cloudless winter sky.

Pais returned with two steaming cups of cocoa. She handed me a mug then sat down. "So what is it this time? Dream you were a mouse?"

"Don't make it sound like you're some psychiatrist or something. I just haven't been feeling, you know, since my grandpa died, I haven't felt … I've been thinking a lot about dying, you know."

"Yeah, but it's been a while now. I know you've been feeling down, but Eliza it's time to face things again. Life goes on."

"I know, but …" I looked up at the moon where a wispy white interloper had nestled by its side. "See that cloud there, Pais? You know how when you look out your window at night and the sky's so big and dark that all you can see is the moon way up high? And next to it is a cloud, like that one there? And you think, how, out of the whole dark sky, is there only one cloud and it's next to the moon? What you don't know is that there are all these other clouds up there, too. Thing is, you just see that one near the moon because the moon lights it up. See? So you think those other clouds aren't there at all, that they don't exist, but they do. You just don't notice them."

I sipped the cocoa. Its thick chocolaty creaminess traveled down my throat, warming me from the inside out. "Sometimes I feel like all those other clouds. Like the very darkest place in the sky."

"Eliza, it's not that bad, is it? Don't you think you're exaggerating? You didn't even hang out that much with your grandpa?"

"It's not just that, just him," I turned toward her. "I'm really feeling down, Pais, and I'm really scared. I don't want to die!"

"What do you mean, die? Is there something you're not telling me? Are you sick?"

"No, no, I'm talking about just dying because, because of just nature or whatever."

"Oh, like when we're – old? Well, Eliza, in case you hadn't noticed, we're still in junior high. Death's a long way off. You don't need to worry about that now. Think about being here, about your Life, about what you want to do with it. Just live day to day, or you'll miss out on all of the little moments that make up your life."

"Day to day, huh?"

"Are you sure nothing else is bothering you?"

"Isn't death enough?"

She didn't answer me, just kinda smiled.

I stared out the window into the dark blue sky. The scattered stars sparkled like a jewelry case of diamonds. The twinkling gems appeared happy, content to rest upon the night's heavenly blanket. Maybe when we died, we joined the stars, sparkling above the world, watching over it like guardian angels. Maybe Grandpa sat up there now, watching me.

I shivered.

"Pais, are you afraid to die?"

"No, I think, in a way, it's kind of exciting. We really have no idea what happens to us. It must be something adventurous, something really amazing, so amazing, that our minds can't imagine it. That's why I believe that the more good we do here on earth, the more wonderful death will be for us." She sipped her cocoa.

"Wonderful, huh? Do you think there's a Heaven?"

"Yep." No doubt or quaver.

"Where then?"

"Where's Heaven?" I nodded, and Pais bit her top lip then said, "I guess it's in our imaginations, beyond our reach.

Remember that time by the lake last summer when you said we won't know what happens to us until we die?"

"Yeah."

"Well, you're right. But if we're going to worry about it while we're alive, we need to think positively. In fact, we shouldn't *worry* about it, but *wonder*. Wonder and imagine. Death can be what you want. Worrying about tomorrow's math test tonight does no good. It doesn't help you know the math. It doesn't help you feel good. So why do it? Study, understand it, ask questions, then just trust that you will do your best. And if you don't pass – it's not the end of the world.

"I mean, I know you're thinking I get A's all the time, so how could I say that" (true, exactly what I was thinking) "but really, worse things happen in Life than failing a test. So if you think you will fail, and you worry and don't get much studying done, you might just talk yourself into it. But if you study and really take an interest in what you've learned and think positively, then you'll pass. That's what I do all the time."

And Paisley's never failed anything in her Life.

I looked at her pale face. For a moment, she looked so old. She sat motionless, her dark brown eyes not even blinking and that *that's just the way it is* smile spread close-lipped across her face. Everything was so open-and-shut for her.

"Well, I guess I better get back now. I don't want Mom or Dad opening my door and seeing an empty bed." I finished my last drop of cocoa, the best part with all the chocolate and sugar clumped at the bottom. I rescued the final bits with my finger, licked it and set the mug down. "Thanks for the cocoa - and the talk."

She opened the window and helped me reach the prickly tree. "Good luck on the test, Eliza. See you in the morning? 7:30."

"Okay." Quickly down the frozen tree, I ran across the yard, through the gate, up our trellis, and back into my warm bed before I could even think about my friend's wise words.

I was much more tired, too, since the escape, so I easily rolled over and fell asleep, dreaming about triangles, square roots and maybe a star or two.

I woke up in the morning. Here on earth. I even passed my math test. I slept better after Paisley's midnight-talk. She didn't say anything that amazing, but sharing deep thoughts with my best friend calmed my inner babblings. A bit.

After all, I can only worry about things so far. Then I just tire of my own repetitive thoughts.

30

MORE WHISPERS AND A CHANCE ENCOUNTER

You never know what each day will bring. Nothing is guaranteed. Nothing is predictable. Take today. This morning Mom wanted to go to church. Had I not joined her (okay, so I was a bit reluctant), this day, this Sunday, January 14, might have continued on being an ordinary, boring same old Sunday.

But it wasn't.

As I readied for our outing, I began pondering - obsessing really – about Life. Surprised?

Of all the things that will happen, I sometimes wonder what will really matter in the very end. What will count, be remembered, and what will be brushed aside like dust in an art gallery?

Would it have really made any difference in the end if I had shown Billy Gold mine in his tent? Will it really matter that we saved those mice? Would it have made any difference at all if I had never climbed a tree or if Dad hadn't cut down my maple? Would things have been any different if Benjie hadn't run after that ball?

And does it really matter that I help Paisley with this organization? Is anyone out there keeping score?

What's important? Who do I listen to?

"Concentrate on your purpose on Earth, Eliza,"

confidently shares Eric. "Think about Life and why you're here."

Pais believes she knows what that purpose is for me (coincidentally the same for her): "Help those less fortunate, like the animals."

Still, it's Grandpa whose words ring truest: "The most important thing of all is to believe in you, listen, trust in what you know to be true."

Really, I think they are each saying the same thing. All three have at one time told me to listen to my instincts, my intuition.

Pais calls this the voices of the Goddess. Eric agrees. Grandpa, well, I think he'd agree too.

So, intuition, instincts, whispers and quiet voices – they are each divine messages? Am I supposed to figure all of this out now?

Personally, I think my teen years will be better spent looking for love. Boyfriends. I haven't had one yet, and there are only so many more days I can take staring at Joe Basketball before I just run up and kiss him myself!

Yet I can't shake the itch of those whispers. Something tells me I need to listen. Something tells me, Joe Basketball may have to wait.

Sunday morning, January 14, 1979, 13, church

So Mom felt compelled to sit in a church today. It had been years for her, but since Grandpa, it's what she needed. She asked me to join her, and since my plan is to get closer to Mom, I washed my face and changed my shirt. Didn't someone say something about being clean means being closer to God?

As I sat among the regulars inside the stained-glass building staring skyward toward the enormously high ceiling, I couldn't help but feel its hollowness. Despite people filling the church, it felt empty and cold.

I gazed passed each obedient face as painted mouths repeated hymns and prayers, and unsteady voices sang songs. Some voices rang proud, others quavered over off-key notes. Eyes glazed, staring blankly at the preacher and every now and then at one another. The women in new silk dresses glanced pityingly at those in recycled church attire.

As Reverend Allison spoke, his accusatorily booming voice filled the hollow cavern before us. His spindly fingers itchingly twitched at his lectern, craving just one more cigarette before the service ended. Restless children imitated his impatient digits as they squirmed back and forth in uncomfortable wooden pews. A man with a message, the Father preached to his congregation against the evils of child abuse and neglect, this week's sermon.

"He who scorns a child scorns himself. He who abuses that love of God…"

I squirmed like an 8-year-old. "Mom, how long?"

"Shh."

"Mom, this doesn't have anything to do with us."

"Shh."

Bored. My thoughts turned to that box in the front hall. At this point, I'd decided it contained Grandpa's stuff, maybe even items from Mom's childhood.

"Mom, tell me what's in the box," I pleaded in the softest whisper possible.

"Maclyn. We're here to listen to Reverend Allison. Now, settle down. Maybe you can learn something." She adjusted her skirt, recrossed her legs, moistened her lips and palmed at her coiffed do – the entire time her gaze never left the pulpit.

I retreated and set my attention around the congregation. I looked for Suzy and quickly spied the bright pink bow in a front pew.

Feeling better that I wasn't the only teen put through this torture, I smiled and glanced to my right for a moment.

Oh, God! I swallowed and instantly turned forward. I pretended to find interest in the sermon.

"Blah, blah ... and times ... blah ... children ... blah, blah." It was useless; I couldn't concentrate. Had he been here this whole time? Joe Basketball sat only three people to my right.

I swallowed again, looked down at my Keds, finding a new hole near the big right toe then slowly turned my head toward my Junior High obsession. He caught my eyes and waved. Was he looking at me? Was he hoping I'd look back at him?

My heart pounded so loudly, I didn't hear Mom telling me to sit up. The forever-sermon had ended, and Reverend Allison reminded his congregation about the indoor hotdog barbeque later that day, and not to forget the animal shelter fund or indeed the church's own monetary needs.

Postures fell, sighs of relief echoed off the sky-high ceiling as the service ended and people filed out, smiling at familiar faces, quickly turning their spiritual thoughts back to worries about Sunday night's dinner or getting the car tuned. The painted women pushed tired children toward shiny cars as men loosened their ties and talked business or finalized bets on the day's big game.

The choir sang an unfamiliar tune. Some joined in, most hugged neighbors and began exiting.

I felt a tug at my sleeve. I turned to the right. Joe Basketball.

Frozen, I couldn't find my voice at all.

"Hey, Mac, fancy meetin' you here," he chirped, his bright tooth-filled smile blinding me.

"Yeah," I replied oh so elegantly.

"Well, uh, happy Sunday." He opened his arms. I stood frozen.

He moved in.

I thought I was going to faint.

His right arm touched me first then his chest to mine then his left arm wrapped around and he embraced me for days.

No? Okay, a moment then.

"Happy Sunday, Mac." He let go.

Had I hugged him back? Had I even replied, "Happy Sunday, Joe"? Probably none of the above. In fact, I'm hoping I didn't say *Joe* because that's not even his name. That's my code name. By the time I returned to reality, I noticed his back walking toward the center aisle, joining other Sunday regulars, returning that smile, my smile, to each. A handshake, his hand, reaching, holding others.

Then, I felt it. A warmth, a tingle, a flush across my face, and a smile. Joe Basketball said my name. Joe Basketball hugged me.

As I walked out the church with my weary mother immersed in her own private thoughts, I wondered why Mom hadn't taken me here before. If it weren't for Grandpa, we wouldn't have shown up this Sunday. I wouldn't have been sitting three people away from Joe Basketball. He wouldn't have hugged me and said my name.

I reached our old blue station wagon and fingered the wood paneling across the passenger door while Mom accepted sentiments for Grandpa from other costumed women. A smile sewn to my face, I observed the sky. The fiery sun edged further upward the vastly ascending landscape.

I paused. Days begin and end and begin again. Each day arrives brand new, something that has never happened before. Every now and again the routine might change, might not.

Today it did.

It's a whisper, right, Grandpa, I thought. Love, God – they're not separate. I don't need to choose. I can listen to whispers and believe, and I can find love. Sometimes it's just sitting three people away and meets you in a warm embrace with a bright toothy smile and a gentle hello.

Sadly, I watched the glowing red ball disappear behind the towering church, leaving only its pink reflection to fill the morning sky. I mourned its departure but only for a moment because I soon discovered that if I stood on my tiptoes, I could watch this warm friend disappear one more time.

The higher I stretched, the more I could see, and the more times I could spend gazing at this mighty light.

31

EXPLAINING THE UNEXPLAINABLE

Having survived church and Joe Basketball all in the same day, I'm feeling pretty powerful. So last night after dinner, I asked Mom if she could open up that big cardboard box.

"Tomorrow, Maclyn. We will open it up tomorrow night." At least we've got a date.

First, I need to share today's earlier events. Today, on our way home from school, Pais and I experienced something I can't quite explain.

Monday, January 15, 1979, age 13, walking home

We've passed the church everyday these past two years on our way home from school, but yesterday was my first actual time inside. I told Pais about the visit, Joe Basketball and Mom's promise to open the box.

"So your dream boy goes to church, huh?" The battle began.

"Yeah," I replied, having anticipated Paisley's judgment. "Well, he was there yesterday. I don't know if it's a habit. Maybe he just happened to be there the same day I happened to be there. And –"

"And he wished you 'Happy Sunday'? Like everyone else?" she interrupted.

"Well, yeah," I offered. "So what if he goes to church, anyway. He's a nice guy."

"We're nice, Eliza, and we don't go to church. Nice and church are not married." Oh so Paisley.

"Haven't you ever been a little curious about the inside? It's kind of pretty. Big, spooky maybe, but pretty, too."

"Yeah, I'm curious," she surprised me. "Let's check it out."

I glanced at my watch and noted the second hand inching past Wonder Woman's ankle. Nearly 3:30. "Okay."

We turned the corner, heading toward the brownstone building and a deserted mid-day street. It had rained heavily all day, and dark ominous clouds filled the afternoon sky. The Allisons lived around the corner where the reverend took callers outside church hours. He used to see people inside the church. That was about five years ago, but something had happened that spooked him so much, he changed the visits to his house.

Reverend Allison never told anyone exactly what had happened. Suzy always bragged that a ghost lived there, and that it had stolen her father's sermon, hid his books, and generally caused mischief. Hard to believe that the reverend only ventures inside his own church when it's filled with people.

His office sits behind the church. That's how we got in. Pais pried open the window and we crawled inside. Climbing carefully over the Reverend's desk, we crept through his door into the church.

Breaking and entering into a church seemed to be events that cancelled each other out, I rationalized.

The empty pews and unnatural silence sent chills up my arms. Pais and I sat down in the front pew.

"It's a lovely church, really, don't you think, Pais?"

"Yes. Lovely windows. Lovely light. Hmm, quite peaceful."

"Okay, let's go," I suggested as I started to stand. It didn't quite feel as warm and welcoming as it did about 24 hours ago when someone hugged me and wished me "Happy Sunday".

"Oh stop, Silly. Sit down. Listen. Close your eyes. Feel something?"

I closed my eyes, trying to listen over my heart's pounding. I scooted closer to Paisley. "I don't feel anything," I said, opening my eyes.

"No? Hmm. Well, I think someone's watching us."

For a moment, I thought Reverend Allison had found us out. He wouldn't be mad, though. Come on, two girls sneaking into a church just to sit there?

"I don't see anyone."

Just then we heard what sounded like something falling in the back of the church. "What was that?"

"I don't know," I instinctively grabbed Paisley's hand. "Let's go."

"No, come on," Pais released my hand, stood and walked down the aisle toward the reverend's office.

"Where're you going?" I whispered as I stood, looking around then following closely behind. "Don't leave me here."

"Shh."

Just as we were about to open the office door, we heard it again. "Someone's in there, Pais, let's go.... There, we can go out the front door. Come on, let's –"

"Shh." She turned the knob then slowly pushed open the door. "Who's there?" she asked calmly, as if opening the door to a girl scout selling cookies.

"Ahh!" I screamed. A small furry something ran past our feet and out the office.

"Eliza! Look, you left the window open," Paisley scolded, taking no notice of what I thought must have been a rat, or a mouse, scampering under the church pews.

I remembered having closed the window because I looked outside as I did it. In fact, I was positive. "I closed it, Paisley. I'm sure of it. Actually, when I locked it, I accidentally knocked over a can of pencils. See?" I pointed to a half-dozen golf pencils scattered on the ground.

"Hmm. Are you absolutely sure about that? Look, the window is open, and we're the only ones here, unless..."

"Unless what?"

"Unless someone else is here."

Oh, brilliant, I thought. Well, of course, someone else had to be here. That mouse didn't open the window. Maybe ghosts did live inside the church, or worse yet, maybe Reverend Allison was here watching us. Terror struck me, the kind of terror that rises up from nowhere thrusting completely crazy and illogical thoughts into your head.

"Pais, maybe Revered Allison is here and he's going to kidnap us," I whispered, moving closer to her side. "Or, someone, whoever spooked Reverend Allison away. That could explain the unexplainable."

"Who are you all of a sudden, Nancy Drew? Give me a break. Reverend Allison's no kidnapper. He's just a crazy preacher trying to scare people into going to church. He's not a child stealer."

How does she do this? She acts as if there's no way she could be wrong then say something to prove she's a little crazy.

"Could be the ghosts."

"Ghosts? Ghosts seem more likely to you than a kidnapper?"

"Yeah, actually, it does." Again with confidence. Then she shushed me and pulled her finger up to her ponytail twisting her hair around it as she bit her top lip. Paisley in serious thought. "Now, let's think about this for a minute."

She looked around the messy office, opening cupboards and drawers - basically snooping.

"What are you looking for?"

"I'm not really sure, but I'll know it when I find it." Now who was Nancy Drew?

"Oh, come on, Pais, who cares. Let's go. This is just like in the movies. Two teenagers in an empty church, they hear a noise, see an open window, they decide to look around. Doesn't that sound stupid?"

Ignoring my last comment, she inquired, "You're positive you locked the window? You didn't just close it, you locked it. Right?"

"Absolutely." My impatience brought forth simple answers for my sleuthing friend.

"Then someone else has to have opened it. And they must be hiding here somewhere because the door was shut just now."

"So."

"So – so that mouse ran out. Where did the mouse come from? Did someone hide in a place where the mouse had been, so that when we opened the door, the frightened mouse ran towards the opening?"

"Okay, if it's a ghost, a ghost isn't going to take up space."

"What? What's convinced *you* it's a ghost, and how do you know they're invisible? Have you ever seen one?"

"Exactly."

"Huh? Eliza!" Now Pais was the one losing patience. She shook her head and mumbled something under her breath then walked out of the office. I stood there for a moment before I realized I was alone, or that maybe I wasn't.

"Hey, wait for me," I yelled as I ran after her.

"Shut the door."

"Why?"

"Look, just shut the door, Eliza, okay?" The mother tone. Another clear indicator of her growing impatience.

"Okay." As I began to pull the door shut, I glanced up at the window. It was closed and locked. I left the door and ran up to the altar where Pais was investigating things. "Pppais?" I stammered.

"What is it now?" she asked annoyed.

"Did you lock the window there?"

"No. In fact, you'd better go do that so no one else gets in."

"But, Pais ... well, it's ... someone's ... the window – it's locked. Someone locked it." I grabbed her arm and moved in closer.

She stepped back, "Are you sure?"

"Yes, of course I'm sure. Go look for yourself." Regretting my words as soon as I'd said them, not wanting her to leave me but not wanting to follow her back to the office either.

Pais cast a wary eye on me, "What are you up to, Eliza? Is this some sort of joke? Are you making fun of me? What have you put in that office?"

"Nothing. Go see for yourself." Again regretting my offer.

She grabbed my arm. "Then you come with me."

We both cautiously approached the reverend's office door. It was shut. "Hey, Pais, I never closed the door. When I spotted the locked window, I ran up to get you."

"Maybe the wind blew it shut. Come on. We're together." She turned the knob. "Hmm, that's funny. The door's locked. Now, how can that be? Look, there's not even a key-hole here."

"Maybe it locks from the inside."

"Maybe. But then, if it does, then that means ... somebody ... or something ... is in there." Was Paisley Park scared?

"Oh, God, come on, Pais, let's just go!" I pulled her arm.

"No, shh. Listen." We put our ears to the door.

"I don't hear anything."

"Shh ... there, did you hear that?"

"What?"

"Listen."

"I don't hear anything, Pais, let's just go." Then I heard what sounded like a baby crying. "What was that?"

"I'm not sure. But it sounds like a cat." She turned the knob again. This time it moved all the way. It wasn't locked. "Come on," she invited nervously as she took *my* hand this time. We peeked around the door. On Reverend Allison's desk sat a cat.

"That must have been why that mouse ran out. The cat."

"Yeah, but that doesn't explain the whole window thing." Paisley moved slowly toward the cat. "Hey, little girl, whatcha doin? Look how pretty you are." Paisley stroked the orange cat's soft fur. The furry feline purred and nuzzled Paisley's arm. Pais lifted its collar. "It's the Allison's cat. She must've been here the whole time. Maybe she got locked in."

"Maybe they keep her here to get rid of the mice."

"Hmm, good point. Now that's weird." I followed Paisley's gaze up toward the window.

"Okay, I swear it was shut. I am positive. So positive."

A chilly breeze blew in through the open window. "Did you lock it?"

"No, that's what I've been saying. I never touched it since we first came in. But when I came back to close the door, it was shut."

"Was it locked, though?"

"Well, yeah, I think."

"You think or you know?"

"I don't know, for sure. I'm all confused with the mouse and the cat and everything. I just know for definite that it was shut. But if it was locked ..." I tried to remember. "I don't know."

"Well, it doesn't really matter. I think the wind probably pushed it shut, like the door. And the cat could've pushed it open. It must have a way of getting in and out of the church."

"But I know I locked it when we first came in."

"Yeah, that's the puzzling part." Suddenly, a bitter gust of wind blew past us, slamming the door and window shut. The orange cat meowed loudly and ran around the room as though chasing something - or even being chased.

"What's up with that cat?"

"Yeah, weird, huh?"

"Oh, God, Pais. I bet it's running around crazy because there's a ghost in here. Come on, please, let's go. Let's just go out the front door. I've had enough Nancy Drew."

"Me, too," Paisley agreed. "But we can't go out the front. Someone might see us, and we have to get our backpacks."

"Let's just leave them."

"No, you go get them. I'll wait here."

"Me? Why me? Let's go together."

"Just go. I'll stand right here by the door watching you."

I swallowed, peaked into the large church area. The altar seemed twice as far away now. I looked up toward the ceiling, searching for a little courage. I thought of Grandpa. You're here, right, Grandpa?

I smelled his sweater. Did I hear his chuckle?

I smiled.

"What's up with you? Go on, Eliza."

No point in sharing these thoughts with Paisley. I found my courage and ran up to the altar, retrieved our backpacks, and hurried back to Paisley.

"It sure feels like someone's here. Can you feel it, Eliza?"

"Yeah, I do." But this time I wasn't afraid.

We walked back through the office toward the window. Looking all around me, above, to the sides, behind, believing I would see Grandpa. But I didn't see anyone.

We crawled back out the window and ran home. We never really saw any ghosts. At least, I don't think we did.

Out of curiosity, I called up Suzy Allison and asked her the name of her orange cat. She wanted to know how I knew about her cat. She told me that her cat, Timber, had died the year before and the family had buried it behind the church. They never got another one because her dad really wanted a dog instead.

I shared this with Paisley. She said Suzy must've been kidding me. Why, though? I didn't even mention our visit to the church.

Well, I don't care what Paisley says, I stand convinced the cat was a ghost. In fact, part of me thinks it was Grandpa. Why not? Nothing happened to us. The only real scary thing inside that stone building was surely the overactive imaginations of two teenaged girls.

Fear just wipes a big dirty smudge across the world and you miss out on all the beauty and magic. Since Paisley couldn't offer any real answers about today, I have my own. And my own say it was magic, it was Grandpa.

That just feels right.

32

LOVE REQUIRES TRUST

Mom opened the box tonight. Finally. And I couldn't believe what was inside. I'm not sure if it's excitement or anxious wonder that courses through my teenage body.

Monday Evening, January 15, 1979, still 13, home

"Mac! Come downstairs. Mom wants us all here." I heard the familiar shout from Marc and capped my pen. My English essay could wait.

"Coming!" I shouted back.

The box had been moved from its usual position in the front hall to a room fit for an audience – the living room. Mom gathered the whole family around this monumental cube of cardboard.

Marc and Eric sat on the blue-cord loveseat. Kenny leaned against one arm while Kevin sat on the coffee table. Dad claimed his reading chair, and Mom stood over the box with a knife.

The scene was set.

"Okay, Mac's here, open it up, Mom," Marc's impatience spoke for us all.

"Alright, well, I just want you to know that it's not what you see inside here, it's what you'll hear." Mom's melodrama gave me the shivers. Was there something alive in there?

She stared at us. "Want me to help you slice it open, Honey," Dad asked.

"No, I can do it." Do it, do it! I wanted to shout.

She extended the knife along one seam and sliced through the clear sticky packing tape like she was serving cake. Another seam separated, and now the middle. Mom set down the knife and slowly peeled back the flaps of the box.

Carefully, she reached in and pulled out a large blob wrapped in newspaper. I imagined it was fragile, made of glass or something. It didn't look alive.

"What's that?" I asked.

"Wait," Dad interrupted. He walked over and helped my mom place the object on the coffee table. Kevin stood up and walked over to me.

Kenny peeked inside the box. "There's some other stuff, too, Mom." She looked from Kenny to my dad then reached into the box. Out came a stack of what looked like letters.

"What're those," I asked, still waiting for the answer to my first question.

"Looks like letters," Kevin offered.

"Who're they from, Mom?" asked Kenny.

"Are they from Grandpa?" Eric later told me he at first thought they were love letters to Grandma, but then he realized those would be something she'd want to have in New York.

"They're letters," Mom confirmed. "They're from … they're to, to Grandma and Grandpa. They're pretty old, and …" We could tell she was struggling for the right words.

"They're from my sister. From Ella. And, some, some are from, from her mother." Silence. The room was silent. Each one of us stared at Mom, at the letters.

"Ella? Who's Ella?" I asked.

"Wait. You have a sister? And she's living with *her* mother?" Eric interrupted. "Not Grandma then. This Ella, she's not Grandma's?"

At some point, everyone had stood up and now we surrounded my mother, moving in on her like little animals, each trying to get to one of the letters.

"Okay, guys, sit down, leave Mom some room. Let her tell the story." Dad motioned to each of us. Kenny and I sat on the floor. "Honey, you sit here."

Mom took Dad's reading chair. Dad stood behind Kevin who had taken up the arm that Kenny'd been resting on earlier.

"This is crazy," I whispered to Kenny.

"Tell me about it," he replied.

Mom fingered the letters, which were wrapped with yellow string. There looked to be about a dozen or so envelopes. I could see a postage stamp on the top one, so I figured these were letters Ella had mailed to Grandpa.

Wow, Mom had a sister.

"When I was little, seven or eight, I remember meeting Ella. She was about a year older than me and talked very fast. We were at a carnival or fair or something. Grandma wasn't there. It was me and Bert and Grandpa. Ella walked up to Grandpa and gave him a big hug. The lady with her shook my hand and Bert's. She was Ella's mother." Mom turned the packet of letters around in a circle.

I looked over at Eric. He was staring into his lap and fiddling with the stitching on the leg of his jeans.

Mom looked at me. "Maclyn, you know how you've always wanted a sister? Well, I had one, but I didn't. Grandpa had an affair, and Ella is his daughter. Grandma never knew. Bert and I didn't know at the time we met her who she was, but we never forgot her.

"I found these letters in Grandpa's things. They're from Ella. She lives in L.A." Tears streamed down my mom's cheeks.

"Can we meet her? Don't you want to see what she looks like now?" I asked.

Mom sighed. She wiped at the tears on her cheeks and

smiled. "Ella has her own family now, Maclyn. She has two boys about your age. Twins. She didn't get married until she was 30. Took her awhile to meet the right man."

"Do the letters say she wanted to meet you?" Eric inquired, a bit boldly I might say.

"I haven't read all of them. I just opened the most recent one because I didn't know what they were. When I read this one," she pulled at the top envelope, "I discovered something I'd always feared. See, Grandpa told me and Bert not to mention Ella to Grandma."

"Grandpa had an affair?" Marc finally caught on.

"Marc!" Dad scolded.

"It's okay," offered Mom. "It's true. Grandpa had an affair."

Words hung in the air. No one moved. Suddenly, the newspaper folded around that blob started uncurling.

Was it trying to get our attention? Grandpa said to listen for him, that he'd be around.

"Eric, I don't know if she wants to meet me, but I think I want to meet her. It's been more than 35 years. If anything, I need to tell her that my dad – her dad – that he's died." Mom slumped back into the chair, hugging the letters to her chest she added, "It's the right thing to do."

I couldn't get over my mom. This was not her thing. Discomfort. I was impressed.

"I'll go with you if you want, Mom."

"Thanks, Honey. We'll see. I don't have her phone number. I'll write her a letter first. Then we'll see."

"So there's some mystery in this family, huh? Pretty cool." Marc was about the only one in the room grinning at this revelation.

Eric playfully swiped at Marc's head. Marc shrugged and looked confused.

"What's that thing you took out of the box then," Kenny asked, assuming probably like the rest of us that it couldn't be as mind-blowing as Mom finding out she had a sister at age 43.

"Why don't you unwrap it," suggested Mom, not making any effort to move from her chair.

Kenny peeled back the newspaper gently revealing an unusual metal sculpture. It was a flat three-dimensional greenish metallic object, about two-feet wide and maybe two or so feet high.

"It's a tree!" I realized.

"A family tree," Dad clarified.

We gathered around the coffee table. Kenny turned it to face me. The entire tree was made up of several little picture frames inside leaves. There were maybe 20 different photos. Some people I recognized – Grandma and Grandpa, Mom, Dad. Some I didn't – probably my great- grandparents.

"Hey, it's us." I touched the tiny photos of my four brothers and me. I turned to Mom. "Is this Grandpa's? Did he make it?"

"He did, Maclyn," Mom was now kneeling beside me. "He made it for you. It's in his will. He wanted you to hold onto the family tree. He's trusting you with it."

All of a sudden the room grew blurry. Hot tears rolled down my cheeks.

"Wow," I whispered. Mom's arm wrapped around my body.

"Grandpa loved you so, Maclyn, and he knew you loved your tree. He told me one day last fall to put this in his will. He wanted you to take care of it. He said only Maclyn knows how to take care of a tree."

Before I knew it, I was bawling and my mom was hugging me. I was happy, I was sad, I was honored. I was so filled with every feeling imaginable.

Oh, Grandpa, I love you. It *was* you today in the church, I know it. I believe, Grandpa. I believe in you, in me, in everything. Life seems so big sometimes, like a huge desert with no visible paths. I try one direction and think I'm traveling in circles. I've always thought there're no landmarks, just moving tumbleweeds.

But I was wrong.

There are lots of markers. I just need to open my eyes and notice the details in the rocks and bushes to see where I've been. I know that if I listen closely enough, and often, I will hear more each time. Like in the church today. Once I let go of my fear, I sensed you, Grandpa. I sensed safety and love.

Love takes listening. Love requires trust. Love creates belief. Belief brings love.

33

A MIGHTY TREE GROWS INSIDE ME

When Dad cut down my maple tree two weeks before my 13th birthday, I thought he was the cruelest person alive. Terminal disease, he said. Doubtful, I say. I don't need to stop climbing trees to grow up. The Goddess would never make such demands.

I don't climb trees much lately, but that doesn't mean that I'd turn down an invitation. Like I said in the beginning:

No Tree's Too Tall

Eric says we have lived many lives; that we live, die, are born again and so on, and we have been men, women, animals, plants and even rocks. He says we keep coming back until we've learned what we need to know so that we can move on to other forms.

Most of the time, Eric sounds a bit crazy to me. Yet after all I've been through these past months – losing my tree and my grandpa and gaining an aunt – ideas like these cannot be easily dismissed.

Something must explain my instinctive connection to nature, to my maple, the stars, the birds, everything. Not everyone finds the peace I do sitting high up on a tree's solid limb, above everything and everyone.

I know that the more I believe in myself, the easier it will be to make decisions. Like what I should do with my life. At least I hope so. And Goddess, I hope you're listening now, because I am.

Paisley seems too sensible to believe in anything like love, but I know she does. She pretends my babblings about Joe Basketball bore her, but I know she's curious, curious about love.

Pais has never admitted to liking anyone, a boy, I mean. Whenever I bring up the subject, she changes it. I might point out some foxy guy at school, and Pais'll just say something like, "Yeah, okay, well, did you study for the quiz?"

Sometimes, I just want to shake her and say, "Wake up, girl! We're teenagers! This is prime time for falling in love. Aren't you the least bit curious?! Come on, just admit it, boys are cute!"

But it never goes that way. Paisley just stresses the importance of staying focused in school. There'll be time for boys later, she says. Later? I'm not waiting for later. In fact, I'll take now *and* later.

I just want to know what that first real kiss feels like. That first time you kiss someone and they kiss you back, someone who's not your family, someone who you really want to kiss, like Joe Basketball.

I imagine – often these days – what it'd be like, for him to just walk up to me, take my hands, lean towards me and just kiss me, kiss me so that I forget everything and everyone, so that all I feel are his warm lips against mine, his hands squeezing mine, just our bodies standing there on a circle of earth extended out towards the sky with no one else, nothing else around for miles and miles. I imagine. I imagine it's just perfect.

Growing up's not so hard, really. There're a lot of unknowns out there, but there's a lot of good stuff, too.

And, love? Oh, I know it's more than Joe Basketball. Love might be a majestic maple that held me in its tender grasp until I was ready to stay on the ground. Love is friendship, a friendship shared between two people (or a girl and a tree) who have something to give each other.

I often wonder what I gave my maple. Companionship, maybe. Loyalty, for sure. Belief? Be a leaf. Hmm. I guess that's what I gave her most. I believed in her and loved her. Maybe she left because she knew I needed to turn that belief in on myself.

That's what Grandpa was talking about.

Believe.

Someday, I'll be a woman. Grown up. Someday, Paisley will stop fighting the Randy Miles of the world. Someday Dad will realize that his girl can climb trees and still be his little girl. And someday, I will meet the Goddess. Her voice will echo so softly and clearly and gently that it will be like having an old friend return home from a long holiday. Warm and welcoming and familiar.

Of course, I'll never stop climbing trees. Not even when I'm sixty. Because the day I do is the day I stop allowing the magic of possibilities to take hold in my world. So I'll grow up, but not into a grown up. I'll be an adult with adult dreams, but I won't forget what it means to believe.

And I'll have experienced that first kiss - several times. And it will have been warm, and soft and full of possibilities.

As I set down my teenage journal, I look out my bedroom window toward the setting sun. Its pink glow settles along the horizon, one last gift to one more day before it slumbers.

When I was little, I used to think the sun turned into the moon at night. That it dropped inside the ocean or down into the earth at sunset to cool down, dim its shine. Then later that evening, it would rise again into the sky and shine faintly like a night-light casting a quiet glow upon a sleepy world not in need of its bright illumination for a few hours.

I used to stare out my window for hours after sunset, trying to catch a glimpse of it rising back into the sky. But I never saw it. Then I'd leave the window for only a moment, and always when I'd return, there it would be, the happy, white moon.

I asked Dad once how the sun turned into the moon without anyone ever seeing it. He just said, "Oh, that sun's very tricky, but it's bad luck if you see it turn into the moon. It's best not to watch. Best to just let it happen in private."

I believed him for a long time, until I learned in school that they were two different spheres. Then I thought Dad had told me a terrible lie, and I was angry with him. Of course, I soon realized that that was Dad's way of keeping magic in my world, of keeping my world filled with possibilities unimaginable.

So how could this same dad allow the chopping down of my best friend? My beautiful, tall, lush, mighty maple. How could he tell me that I had to stop climbing trees?

Life's contradictions?

I guess Dad is still discovering those possibilities. One day he will realize that I can't ever be a grown-up without a tree to climb. I will turn 14 and 15 and 16, and I will always climb.

I can't stop dreaming, crying, hoping, climbing. Why should growing up stop us from seeing the magic in the world? Some adults just grow up too quickly. Responsibility turns to burden. Future turns to fate. Possibility turns away.

Grandpa, stay with me and guide me. I feel you slipping away like smoke through my fingers. Don't go, Grandpa. Your memory seems already to be fading, so quickly, leaving behind only a trace of you as if you might never have existed at all. You trail like a jet's exhaust that disappears into nothingness before a child's curious and awe-struck eyes.

Oh, I know I'll be okay. I always am because there's always someone around, someone to give advice, or to comfort or even just to lend an ear for listening. No matter where my life takes me, I'll survive. If I fall, I'll get back up. Tree-climbers always do.

A mighty tree grows inside me, Grandpa.

It's there where I'll find my own light and follow it, until it shines brighter and brighter, until I reach its source. And there maybe I'll find you again, Grandpa, or my majestic maple or the Goddess.

Maybe I'll only find me, reflected in that light, shining, glowing, confident, waiting there all along to reveal herself to the world.

This is the end of my story; now it's time to write yours.

ABOUT THE AUTHOR

Ellen Plotkin Mulholland grew up in San Bernardino, California, in the 1970s. After earning her degree in Journalism and English Literature at the University of Southern California, she moved to London. There she bought a green manual typewriter, sat by a window in a Fulham Broadway apartment, and wrote this novel. Today she teaches academic strategies to adolescents and enjoys the delightful exploits of her own kids. Her second YA novel, "Birds on a Wire", is also available from *Logos Publishing House.*

Strike up your own conversation with Eliza at: thisgirlclimbstrees.weebly.com.

Connect with the author at:
facebook.com/thisgirlclimbstrees
facebook.com/authorellenmulholland
twitter.com/thisgirlclimbs

ABOUT THE COVER ILLUSTRATOR

Tim Sunderman is a graphic designer and illustrator who works in the San Francisco Bay Area. His work includes a number of book designs, magazine work, CD, and DVD covers, as well as commissioned paintings. He lives with his artist wife and two daughters in the great harmony of each day, and looks forward to each new creative project. In his work, he tries to avoid computers until there is no other recourse, doing all his own drawing, painting, photography, calligraphy, and even sculptures. But because there is no other recourse than to finish his projects onscreen, he manages in good spirits. To see more of Tim's work, please visit:

http://www.timsunderman.com
For inquiries or just to say "hi", his email is:
info@timsunderman.com

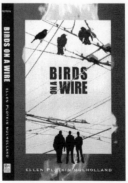